The Supreme Orchestra

DAVID TURGEON

TRANSLATED BY PABLO STRAUSS

COACH HOUSE BOOKS | TORONTO

First English-language edition. Originally published as *Simone au travail* by Le
Quartanier, 2017

Coach House Books acknowledges the financial support of the Government of
Canada through the National Translation Program for Book Publishing, an initiative of the Roadmap for Canada's Official Languages 2013–2018: Education, Immi-
gration, Communities, for our translation activities. We are also grateful for
generous assistance for our publishing program from the Canada Council for
the Arts and the Ontario Arts Council. Coach House Books also acknowledges
the support of the Government of Canada through the Canada Book Fund.

LIBRARY AND ARCHIVES CANADA CATALOGUING IN PUBLICATION

Turgeon, David, 1975-
[Simone au travail. English]
    The supreme orchestra / David Turgeon ; translated by Pablo Strauss.

Translation of: Simone au travail.
ISBN 978-1-55245-375-9 (softcover).--ISBN 978-1-77056-571-5 (EPUB).--
ISBN978-1-77056-572-2 (PDF)

    I. Strauss, Pablo, translator II. Title: Simone au travail. English

PS8639.U7276S5613 2018   C843'.6   C2018-903967-1
                                                 C2018-903968-X

The *Supreme Orchestra* is available as an ebook: ISBN 978 1 77056 571 5 (EPUB)
978 1 77056 572 2 (PDF)

Purchase of the print version of this book entitles you to a free digital copy. To
claim your ebook of this title, please email sales@chbooks.com with proof of
purchase. (Coach House Books reserves the right to terminate the free digital
download offer at any time.)

FAYA

The morning was blizzarding, the gallery deserted. Alban Wouters, proprietor, attended to his ledgers, eye wandering from time to time toward the backdrop of plump grey snowflakes, when an unknown man in a fur-lined cloak of military cut pushed open the door and entered the gallery along with a cruel gust of arctic wind.

Inclement weather sometimes brought just such unknown quantities out of the cold and into his establishment. You could recognize them as the strangers they were by their polite, noncommittal way of sauntering into the gallery's main room and their inquisitive looks as they dutifully eyed the gallery walls with at best an imperfect understanding. Now, Alban Wouters had nothing against unknown quantities per se; confronted with just the right piece, an unknown quantity might metamorphose into a paying client, like larva to butterfly. In such instances, after pondering the work in wonder and at length, the unknown person might turn to the gallery owner and speak.

'How much is that one there?'

Alban Wouters looked up from his ledgers. It was a day for butterfly hunting.

'I'm sorry,' he replied, getting up from his chair, 'that one's sold.'

'Really,' said the man in the pelisse. 'And that one to the left?'

'That one too, I'm afraid,' said the gallery owner, who in the meantime had drawn closer. 'If only you'd been here yesterday.'

Not one to be deterred, the man in the pelisse wordlessly approached another work whose subdued colours had been applied with a studied carelessness, all rectangles and rounded corners, art made to measure for the living room wall of any good bourgeois home.

'It's not your day,' said Alban Wouters. 'The show went very well. There's not much left. Perhaps this?' he said, pointing out an underwhelming miniature.

'I don't know,' answered the cloaked man who, after a moment's hesitation, stuttered, 'It feels like ... it just doesn't work as well, that small.'

'You may be right,' echoed the gallery owner, who had often made the very same remark himself, expressed in the same words and sequence.

The mouth of the man in the pelisse betrayed the onset of disappointment. He looked poised to climb back down the ladder, to the rung of unknown quantity. Time for Alban to make his move.

'Have you, by chance, seen our backroom?'

'No,' said the man in the pelisse, apparently unaware the gallery had such an appendage.

I really must fix my signage, the gallery owner thought, an idea translated into audible speech with the remark that he'd heard this comment before.

'The clients think it's private,' Alban Wouters said, putting the man in the pelisse, who had been labouring under the same misconception, at his ease and in the happy company of the gallery's regular clientele.

The man in the pelisse was Fabrice Mansaré, who had that very morning been taken by a powerful urge to decorate his apartment, the kind of urge that percolates for days before bubbling over into action. Why now? Excellent question. One wonders what was on his mind the night before, to cause such a desire to bloom.

But perhaps there's no need for such psychological profundities: perhaps Fabrice Mansaré simply woke up that morning and found his bachelor apartment too large, too beige, altogether too empty. It's true that he received no visitors; wasn't often home; took dinner, lunch, and breakfast out. The apartment offered little to distract him: six shrink-wrapped albums leaning against a high-end stereo; ten mismatched books, gifts in the main; a TV he by and large ignored.

The only art to speak of was a drawing made by his niece, Eugénie, when she was four and a half. It was stuck with a magnet to a fridge 90 percent empty, an appliance as extraneous as everything else in the luxury kitchen of one disinclined to cook.

It was the home of someone who never stays in one place long, the domicile of a diplomat or hit man.

As if to whet his decorative ambitions, Fabrice Mansaré's contact had failed to reach him that morning. With nothing on the agenda and a vague sense of concern, there was little to keep Fabrice Mansaré in an apartment that was, to say the least, ill-equipped to alleviate his boredom. He resolved to go out. And only once he was outside the lobby door did he notice the raging storm. The spectacle of blowing snow was tonic; Fabrice Mansaré, imperturbable. He began walking, batted to and fro by the north winds savagely howling between the skyscrapers of downtown Bruant.

First stop, espresso: he drank his short and piping hot, then headed out to face the elements. Along deserted sidewalks he made slow progress, enthralled by what was a novel experience for him. Second stop, a lighting shop whose wares caught his eye while he was waiting for the traffic lights to turn. Forty-five minutes later he re-emerged in a flurry of heartfelt thanks from a salesman reassuring him that his fixture would indeed be delivered and installed that very afternoon.

Fabrice Mansaré proceeded to visit a Chinese import store, a kitchen shop, a tailor's, and finally Alban Wouters's gallery, where he was eventually shepherded into a backroom that was in fact difficult to find for those not in the know.

In this second gallery he came upon a mosaic of medium-format drawings depicting people of both sexes in states of partial or complete undress, individually and in pairs and sometimes in small groups, in positions of abandon that left little doubt as to the tenor of the moment caught on paper. To be blunt, scenes of the most elegant debauchery. The artist's pencil outlined flesh and faces in a manner that blurred certain areas and traced others in disconnected, vacillating glimpses simulating the effects of movement or unchecked transports of delight. The gallery owner scrupulously avoided any mention of the work's content, focusing resolutely on its formal and commercial properties: oil pastel screen print in blue ink; a run of twenty, hand-numbered by the artist; framing at the client's discretion.

Fabrice Mansaré slowly contemplated one of these, a woman with thick, kinky hair and lips set in an amused pout, slumped on an outline of a couch in nothing but a wrinkled tank top, hand oscillating between her legs, black pupils leaving not a trace of doubt as to her ability to provide for her own pleasure. Fabrice Mansaré intuited another presence, the gaze of the beholder swollen with desire not unmixed with pain. The gallery owner held his tongue, aware these drawings dredged up complex feelings in prospective buyers, from depths not always easy or advisable to plumb.

'This drawing here,' asked Fabrice Mansaré. 'Is it for sale?'

'It is,' the gallery owner confirmed, at a price he specified.

Fabrice Mansaré pulled from the left pocket of his pelisse a little leather-bound notebook. An entry copied from the bottom of the drawing, *Faya Sitting, 18/20*, accompanied by the price, was appended to the list of the morning's purchases, themselves part of an inventory constantly evolving with moves to antipodean cities where he more or less began his life anew. It wasn't a sense of economy that led Fabrice Mansaré to track expenses: it was a game to him.

'When can I pick it up?'

'At the closing,' Alban Wouters informed him. 'In two weeks. You should come. We'll serve drinks.'

'Let me write you a cheque,' Fabrice Mansaré said, and with these words removed from the right-hand pocket of his pelisse a chequebook, on the first page of which he wrote out the requested amount and signed, as per his recent habit, *Charles Rose*.

'Mr. Rose,' said Alban Wouters obsequiously, writing a receipt.

'If you would be so kind as to tell me the date,' said Fabrice Mansaré.

The gallery owner was so kind. The date was memorable: the birthday of Alice, the big sister Fabrice Mansaré had not seen, as he was reminded every time he thought of her, for at least twenty years. Putting this memory aside, he knotted his scarf, buttoned his pelisse, and, with a wave to the proprietor his silhouette disappeared into the last gasp of February.

The next day Fabrice Mansaré heard from his contact, whose vehicle had been put out of commission by the storm, hence the delay. An appointment was made. Work was back on. Two days later, Fabrice Mansaré turned up, with a single carry-on, no more than one hour early, at the Bruant International Airport where, after the usual check-in formalities, he walked right past a lengthy line of travellers and through a doorway marked *Diplomatic Passports*, where we could no longer lawfully follow him.

At that very moment, a woman emerged from that very airport. Back from a symposium in the Mediterranean, she greeted the brown snow under the taxis' tailpipes with a scowl. The sky was hesitating between shades of grey; a cold wet wind forced its way into the gaps of her hastily fastened coat. She hailed a car. The driver helped stow two heavy bags in the trunk, then they merged onto the spaghetti-tangle of highway where the usual thousands of cars collectively idled.

It would be hard to say how old this woman was. Without her cap, the chalky hair crowning a pinkish face that wrinkled slightly in the corners provided less an answer than a new set of hypotheses. There was nothing particularly feminine about her appearance: her no-nonsense mouth, strong cheekbones, and cropped hair could all have belonged to a man. We might flesh out this portrait by mentioning her voice, by turns shrill and gruff; her movements, frequently brusque; or her stature, short. All we can say for sure was that her first name was Simone. Her surname is another story for another time. The taxi, cleaving for better or for worse to the congested highways, covered several kilometres of exurban sprawl before reaching a winding road that bisected fields as if cut out by a child's scissors. It continued to a hamlet of no more than half a dozen homes. Simone bade the driver stop at a white specimen with pretty green trim and dormer windows.

The driveway was unshovelled but a light was on inside. When Simone finally set her two heavy suitcases down in the hall, snow covered her pants up to the knee. A radio warbled in the living room. The smell of tobacco floated in the air.

'Faya?' Simone ventured.

No answer. Already Simone had taken off her boots, hung up her coat, shaken out her pants, and carried her suitcase to her room. She badly wanted a hot bath.

'I'm home,' she said again, still eliciting no response.

Simone's bed was unmade. An overflowing ashtray shared the nightstand with a pile of open magazines and splayed sociology books. Articles of clothing were strewn in the vicinity of a dirty-clothes hamper. The heater spared no expense. An open closet door revealed a standing mirror in which Simone caught sight of her exhausted face.

She undressed, put on a robe whose sleeves she saw peeking out from under the bed, and finally located two slippers before heading back down to the main floor where she tried once again to make herself heard by Faya, who clearly hadn't gone outside since Simone had left town. She found her in the bathtub.

'Oh, it's you,' said Faya.

'I need a bath,' Simone stated. 'Do you think you could?'

'Get out? In this cold? No way.'

'The heat's on full-blast,' Simone observed. 'I asked you not to touch the thermostat. And you're going to shrivel up like a raisin.'

'Like a raisin! Shrivelled up like a raisin!' Faya sang, vaguely in tune with the melody on the radio still crackling in the distance.

'We'll make a fire,' Simone offered.

'Five minutes!' Faya pleaded. 'Five measly minutes. Please!'

'Okay, I'll come back in five,' Simone conceded.

'And leave me the robe,' Faya stipulated.

Simone headed to the living room for a wait certain to exceed five minutes. Night fell. There was wood to be fetched from outside. A pack of cigarettes, not Simone's, but she helped herself. It wasn't that Faya's presence irked her. And yet … And yet …

Simone fell for her models more often than she cared to admit. Men and women both passed through her studio door, where her discretion built a trust she promised herself never to betray. Step by step she proceeded, from preliminary sketches to studies of faces, hands, and feet; then, as her subjects laid themselves barer and barer, she set their bodies down in oil pastel on yellow paper while her dulcet mezzo and easy charm set them at ease.

After more than fair warning, Simone invited her models to take part in scenes of a more intimate nature and immodest, concupiscent bent. At times like these, she loved the way the bodies got away from her, forgetful of the artist's presence, in tête-à-tête or single-handed pleasures. Simone was fond of difficult things; all this lubricious movement she undertook to fix on paper at breakneck speed, with patiently observed sketches for a scaffold.

Not until later, labouring over a final drawing, did Simone conceive for her models an amorous affection that plunged her into that sweetest of dilemmas. This feeling, when it came at all, did so only days later after she had studied her drawings at length to select the best, remembering only then the physical presence of the people who inspired her, and dropping into a curious carnal reverie that, more often than not, remained private. It didn't have that much to do with the success or failure of the drawings – not always anyway. She felt desire for women and for men without distinction, and sometimes also for the couples they formed rather than individual members thereof.

And sometimes, never quite fortuitously, this desire gave rise to an actual love affair, though rarely one that lasted more than a day or two. Sometimes she had to reluctantly put an end to it: no matter how lovely they were, Simone didn't like her affairs to drag on. And then there was Faya.

Faya. Simone couldn't say whether what she felt was love, but it was intense, vexatious, and difficult to extirpate, compounded by the fact that the object of this feeling seemed in no rush to end her tenancy in this home she had moved into over a month ago and now occupied as if it were ever thus and Simone were the interloper.

'Faya, you have to go,' Simone said, too quietly for Faya to hear.

Night kept on falling. Faya was running the hot water again and Simone was readying to storm the tub when the phone rang, as telephones do.

'It's Alban,' announced Alban Wouters. 'I heard you'd be back tonight. I sold another drawing three days ago. No, a new client, never seen him before. Otherwise the gallery's strangely quiet these days. What about you?' Simone told Alban about the unsurprising symposium, some agreeable new acquaintances. And the sea, one never tired of the sea. 'I wonder what I'm doing back here, in the cold,' she said, half-joking. 'Spring is just around the corner,' the gallery owner informed her. 'And how's Faya?' The conversation stumbled on and then Faya appeared in the living room like a genie from a bottle, her skin gleaming, a trail of steam in her wake.

'I have to go,' Simone notified Alban, before returning the black handset to its cradle.

'You promised me a fire,' Faya said.

'Fire, fire,' Simone said. 'Go ahead and make it yourself if you're in such a rush.'

'No, no,' said Faya, throwing on the bearskin that bedecked the couch. 'I'll wait for you.'

They'd seen the bottle of gin through to its conclusion, enjoyed another of rum as an epilogue, wolfed down pasta drenched in olive oil, and exchanged an embrace or three. Faya's lower thighs certainly felt like the softest of silks upon which Simone might hope to rest her tired hands.

And her lover's euphoria was to Simone's ears a music no less sweet for its undertone of bitterness. But biologists have proven the matter beyond a reasonable doubt: only men fall asleep immediately upon orgasm. Long story short, Simone slept poorly. She not only slept poorly but also woke early, altogether too early and long ahead of the tardy winter-morning light she then awaited, in a foul mood, vexed by the utterly indecent hour alleged by her alarm clock, six-fifteen to be precise. And now what?

Nothing doing, no further sleep was forthcoming. Faya opened her eyes to find Simone perpendicular in her rattan chair in the corner of the room, distractedly darkening pages with one hand in a sketchbook she held in the other.

Faya was flattered.

'Should I pretend to masturbate?' she asked, never averse to mixing business and pleasure.

'No,' said Simone, polishing off her sketch with a hint of unnecessary violence in her strokes. 'I was just trying to draw you sleeping.'

'But I'm not sleeping anymore,' said Faya, stretching.

Simone was running out of subjects for her drawings. She'd stopped inviting people over to model. It wasn't that Faya was the jealous type, exactly, but how to put it?

'Pierre-Luc's coming to pick me up soon,' Simone said.

'The hapless suitor!'

'It's for his class,' Simone clarified, pinching the bridge of her nose, 'and do you think you could?'

'Do I think I could what?'

'Nothing,' said Simone.

'Old bat,' Faya said, laughing as she got out of bed, naked as Eve. 'I'll make you dinner tonight if you want. And not pasta and olive oil. I just need a little money. For groceries.'

'Did you leave the house even once while I was gone?' asked Simone quite pointlessly.

Pierre-Luc soon appeared, shovel in hand. 'I did the driveway,' he said when Simone opened the door. 'We'll have to get a move on, though, we're a little late.'

'I'm ready,' answered Simone, already in her turquoise coat. Faya, mute and invisible, had disappeared somewhere in the house.

Pierre-Luc's rusty station wagon pulled out from behind the snowbank and rumbled away toward the art school where he taught drawing. That morning he had taken the time to trim his beard and even dabbed cologne behind each ear. 'I hope it doesn't smell too strong,' he'd fretted. To top it off, he'd made his bed, a chore more often left undone since he broke up with – what was her name again? Simone drew a blank.

Whenever he found himself in Simone's presence, Pierre-Luc was intimidated, incapable of uttering anything but the commonest of commonplaces, and this time was no exception. Syllables and sentences seemed to slip the coil of sense, emerging only as a broken rosary of drab grey beads. But he recovered his customary verve the moment he assumed his position in front of the class. Pierre-Luc's brood sincerely admired their teacher, a model educator with a captivating sense of humour and the ability to acknowledge talent without jealousy and to bestow instruction without condescension. Perhaps it was to have Simone observe him in this state of grace that he so often invited her to his class.

In the theatre of Pierre-Luc's mind, a passionate love story had long been unfolding in which Simone played one leading role and he had dextrously manoeuvred to secure the other, a saga that seemed forever destined to play to an audience of one. But living like this is no life at all. Sometimes Pierre-Luc had to wonder if his fixation wasn't getting the better of him. Which did nothing to stop him from seeking out the company of his muse.

And what did the muse think? The muse was no dupe; she was aware of what was going on, and she shrugged it off. Simone knew all too well that at the heart of every friendship ambiguity lay. There was no avoiding it, except perhaps by staying home all the time – and how sad and small a life was that?

The students stood ready at their easels. Several pairs of eyes lit up at the sight of Simone. An older man entered after them, waved at Pierre-Luc, and, without further ado, disappeared behind a screen whence he emerged five minutes later dressed only in a robe. In the meantime Pierre-Luc greeted his class, needlessly introduced their visiting artist, and gave instructions for the day's exercise. Two latecomers made their way toward their places with excuses mumbled as their teacher was already closing the classroom door.

You'll never learn to draw by observing the bodies of young Adonises and Miss Universes, Pierre-Luc was fond of saying, so he insisted on hiring models of diverse ages and body types, normal folk you might bump into on the street. The man standing before them today was tall, thin, and wan. He had an aura of transparency, as if one might look through him and see every joint and sinew. To further assist the students in their labour of looking, he was standing with his hands on his hips and his torso slightly off-kilter, his left leg bearing all his weight, his back curved to compensate. The students got down to work. Pierre-Luc waited a couple minutes before beginning his rounds; Simone followed suit, counter to his clockwise.

The posture was a tough one to capture, and Simone felt only indulgence for these budding artists struggling with the model's outslung hips and contorted hands. The degree of difficulty varied depending on the beholder's standpoint. From behind, two segments of an obtuse triangle could stand in for each arm. The sideways approach was more arduous, demanding as it did a wholly counter-intuitive perspective on this arrangement of angles.

The students murmured to each other, a sign of the pains they were taking, while Simone offered feedback and encouragement. Too many lines, she chastised one budding artist, find the one that counts and follow it through, start again if you have to. That's good, she complimented another, but a little stiff, maybe soften up the angles? Not bad at all, she praised a third, you really have a feeling for the texture of the skin, well observed – but isn't the rib cage a bit too much? Now that's a great drawing, she said to the next, but it's not our model here at all, imagination's healthy, but respect the exercise. You gave him an odd face, she went on to the next, his gaze isn't that hard, take a good look, he's almost smiling. Ay! Ay! Ay! she exclaimed at the sight of a rather muddled drawing, he's a hirsute man, for sure, but it looks like you just threw hair all over the place, like you're trying to hide the shape of his body.

Two bodies travelling in opposite directions in a single orbit are destined to meet. Pierre-Luc pretended not to see the friendly wink Simone flashed him en passant. Then each continued in their circle.

Simone, unapologetic autodidact, felt ill-equipped to judge other people's drawings. But she did love to watch these tender shoots at work. From time to time she came across one who truly knocked her socks off. In this group there was Sarah-Jeanne Loubier.

'Oh,' said Simone. 'Wonderful!'

Sarah-Jeanne Loubier tucked her head deeper into her shoulders and accepted the compliment without turning around. Simone slipped away again. At any rate she didn't have a thing to say: the drawing was so singular that all comment seemed beside the point.

The model took a few other poses. For the last, Simone drew while the students gathered round to watch and Pierre-Luc did a play-by-play. Not the most congenial set-up, but Simone was a good sport and even answered questions after. Then the students and models packed up and left, it was time, and the teacher invited his guest to grab a bite in town.

They walked in silence to a pizzeria they both liked and in fact went to every time. Sparse cottony snowflakes drifted hesitantly groundward. A table by the window had just opened up. They watched the people walking by outside, each enveloped in their tiny halo of mist.

Pierre-Luc began stammering again – he was powerless to control it, even after Simone gave him a warm look that would have put anyone at ease.

'There's one,' Simone said suddenly, 'who's really something.'

'You mean Sarah-Jeanne,' said Pierre-Luc.

'That's right. It's like she sees everything inside out. Like she's outside looking in, just barely grazing her subject. I don't really know how to explain. How does she do it?'

'Well, I don't know. And I don't dare ask her to change her style. She's stubborn. That's not necessarily a bad thing.'

'It's like she's drawing ghosts.'

'You're right,' Pierre-Luc agreed. 'What a lovely way to put it.'

Pizza came, conversation tapered off.

Pierre-Luc insisted on paying. They parted with a kiss whose tenor might be plotted not far from the midpoint of a median connecting love and friendship, though as we know all too well the path between those particular two points is anything but linear.

An hour later Simone set off on foot. On the way she bought a blouse with white and pale-grey checks, how to resist such a sale? The boutique's bag alone was chic enough, and it wasn't without pleasure that she scurried down to the port where a cruise ship and two icebreakers were moored. The north wind tickled her cheeks. Then she climbed into a tram that would take her to the terminus, Porte du Midi. There she procured a few bottles of wine and took refuge in a café, awaiting her order while admiring the afternoon's purchase. She saw her bus, paid, left the restaurant, and was home by four.

A crepuscular house greeted her: it was that time of year when day cowers briefly and then beats a quick retreat. Faya wasn't there; at least, her jacket and boots had taken leave. A cursory inspection of the fridge told Simone that no groceries had been purchased;

would she not have done better to take matters into her own hands? She removed a few layers and headed toward the living room fireplace to rekindle yesterday's coals. This mission accomplished, Simone stretched out on the couch, took off her reading glasses, and flipped through a few magazines. With a touch of coquetry she donned her new blouse and admired herself in the bathroom mirror.

This is the kind of piece, she thought, bemused, that Faya's sure to snap up. Five-thirty rolled around. Faya, Simone thought, will surely be here soon. They must have just missed each other. Faya's reading materials, mostly borrowed from the Bruant Public Library, were spread out all over the small living room table: *Architecture and Utopia*, by Gustave Alexis Pauk; *The Third World and After: The Political Economy of an Awakening*, by Limane Vieira; *Functions of Art in Emerging Societies*, by Teresa Sliman, and *Beyond Misunderstanding: Feminism and Politics in the Era of Revolutions*, by Leanne Boole – seminal works all, covered in a mushrooming overgrowth of Post-It notes dense with handwriting. Simon flipped through at random. At six she decided there was no point waiting for her aperitif after all. At 8:17, after single-handedly emptying a bottle of Chablis, Simone inspected the pantry and resigned herself to another plate of pasta and olive oil. Still no sign of Faya. She ate without much appetite, at once worried and annoyed that she felt thus.

At 2:28 a.m., Simone awoke to a kerfuffle below. A door closed; then laughter, whispering, clanking of bottles and glasses, what sounded like a drawer opening and shutting. Simone recognized Faya's laugh, and in response the voice of a man – no, two. She heard old floorboards creak under percussive footsteps on the main floor, heading toward the living room where, who knew, a few coals perhaps smouldered still. Someone closed the living room door, and of what then ensued only a muffled version reached Simone's ears. She spent several minutes with her head under a pillow, which blocked out noise imperfectly, and with eyes wide open she listened, what else could she do? The sounds came into focus. The fireplace grille was squeaking. Enthusiastic yelps could be heard, followed by Faya's calls for silence. Then one man began to recite a text that rapidly garnered *bravi* from his audience. My collection of erotica, Simone surmised. The reading dragged on. Simone couldn't quite recognize the text – she hadn't read those for a while, and it wasn't the type of writing whose every sentence stayed etched in your mind. She then became aware of rumblings of another nature, closer in register to moaning, and that's when she remembered the earplugs in her handbag that lay, as chance would have it, on the chair next to the bed.

Simone was woken again at 5:38, this time by the creaking of stairs on which someone was treading, quietly and carefully, up to the second floor. Faya came into the bedroom, got undressed, slipped into bed, and nestled up against Simone in a cloud of exogenous odours: beer, marijuana, mansweat.

'I didn't know you were here,' she lied in a cooing voice into Simone's ear. 'You should have joined us. I even brought one back for you.'

Fabrice Mansaré took advantage of his layover in Port Merveille to send his big sister a birthday card. With a little luck, his missive would reach its destination that very day. Fabrice Mansaré couldn't speculate. For all he knew, his sister might not live in Neudorf anymore. *Give Eugénie a kiss for me,* he wrote in postscript, dreaming of the niece he'd never met in the flesh and knew only through a yellowed drawing, as he entrusted his envelope to the good graces of the international post.

He then boarded his plane, with a brand-new sports bag slung over his shoulder from which, once seated, he extracted a spy novel he proceeded to read not without amusement until they landed. Upon arrival he strode unchecked through customs and walked purposefully to the multimodal station where he waited for the train downtown. He didn't think he was being followed.

Once home, he laid his bag down on his bed and sorted his things: clothing was placed back in the closet, the book rejoined its brethren on the shelf, the drawing of his niece who was no longer four years old enlivened the fridge door. An envelope stamped CONFIDENTIAL went back into an unremarkable briefcase.

Though somewhat exhausted, Fabrice Mansaré remained determined to complete his mission. He picked up his briefcase, changed his clothes, and went back outside. It was almost noon. As he pushed open the lobby door, a black sedan pulled up in front of the building. Two gruff men in black suits stepped out. The driver took up his post and stood, unmoving, at the vehicle's side, keeping Fabrice Mansaré in the sights of his dark glasses. The other man opened the back door without a word.

'Get in, please,' said a phlegmatic voice from the back seat. Fabrice Mansaré complied, without betraying any particular emotion. Three doors closed, the two last in perfect synchrony. The car started.

'I was on my way to the bank,' noted Fabrice Mansaré.

'We'll drop you off,' said the small man who'd enjoined him to get in the car. 'You were able to meet with Sorgue.'

'Yes,' said Fabrice Mansaré, elaborating only with a tap on his briefcase.

'You should lie low for a few weeks,' said the young phlegmatic man. 'People have been talking since you left. Let's not make it any worse. And since you're going to the bank anyway,' he added, handing Fabrice Mansaré a small black case.

'There it is. Of course,' said Fabrice Mansaré when he saw the contents. 'How'd you get it? Wait. It's the next left,' he informed the goons. 'Don't tell me,' he said quietly to the short phlegmatic man. 'I'll take care of it. Could you drop me off at the next light?'

There was a safety deposit box in Charles Rose's name at the Federal Bank of Commerce, where Fabrice Mansaré was welcomed warmly. After depositing the briefcase and small case, he left empty-handed. The sun was very bright, provided you stuck to the side of the street that followed the axis of its rays, and that was what Fabrice Mansaré did, until he realized he hadn't eaten anything since morning.

He made his way into a nearly deserted restaurant in Chinatown. Fabrice Mansaré asked to be seated at the back.

The menu was bounteous in French, even more so in the original. He ordered in Cantonese, steamed hairy crab though it was out of season, and ate it down without a word.

But his mind was racing. A dormant few weeks, he thought to himself, and he was unsure what they had cooked up for him. He thought about Alice's birthday eight days from now, a date supposed to remind him of something, but what?

We believe the fine art of waiting can be accessible to any old johnny-come-lately; nothing could be further from the truth. Waiting is a martial technique lost to the mists of time, acquired only with the greatest of difficulty.

It's not a matter of distracting oneself, but rather of plunging wilfully into the very heart of boredom, simulating it if need be, to perfect the training regimen and trigger the ominous peripeteia that takes us into that state of reclusion and sensory deprivation – and, while you're at it, low-intensity torture – all things it's so much easier to just choose not to think about.

Fabrice Mansaré spends several hours of each day like this, behind drawn curtains, seated on an ordinary chair, methodically clearing his mind. He classifies the ideas that occupy his mental space, attempting to control their nature and rate of flow. Certain matters of the kind that normally escape our vigilance – song choruses, nursery rhymes, insistent leitmotifs – he diligently evacuates and laboriously replaces with others, apparently more rational and ostensibly easier to control, like the creation of an algorithm, the drawing of a map, or the logistics of a rescue operation. But such material soon runs out. Fabrice Mansaré is concentrating on not thinking of anything, convinced that therein freedom lies. Does it, though? Because after a long and very real period of mental respite, something starts creeping its way up, those old, sticky obsessions and confused, poorly lit scenes Fabrice Mansaré knows are part of his past life, buried in a loam packed far too loosely, as if with the express intent of ensuring that he'd be haunted forever. And, instead of chasing them away, the infinitely receptive Fabrice Mansaré directs his dim projector at them, casting ever more light on this dusty scene, patiently conjuring back to life, back into a thorny form, a parody, a gaze he's known before and that, with enough time, he just might expand into an almost complete face, or perhaps a texture of skin he recalls frequently caressing and which, in his memory, is among the most unimpeachably soft things he has ever been blessed to touch; and perhaps, on days when he has truly achieved heightened perception, a state of clarity, what appears to him are colours, copper highlights dappling dark skin. A sudden green flash lights up this vast sad gaze and there emerges, dug up from a forbidden stratum of his memory, that skin's sharp fragrance.

Fabrice Mansaré shudders. It's five o'clock. He's cold.

No, he's hot. The thermal stimuli continue to contradict each other, until they reach consensus: hot on the outside, cold on the inside. Where is the opposite? His naked body seems to be covered in a viscous liquid, and seminal fluid is smeared across the head of his erect cock, which he grabs and satisfies without further ado, a matter of hygiene.

The curtains, once open, show a grey street where taxis and people hurry by on their way home from work. Motors rev in response to the call of the traffic lights. Horns honk. Evening falls. Fabrice Mansaré turns on a little light.

Renée came back from the storeroom with a few boxes of glasses. 'We'll need more,' she thought out loud, laying the glasses in a straight row on a long table draped in white, 'we broke a lot last month, we're almost out.'

Alban Wouters raised his head. 'Really? You're right, the glasses, I'll go buy some more before the people get here.'

'You'll have to hurry,' Renée said, 'it's starting in just over an hour.'

Alban Wouters checked the clock, a circle marked by four black lines that only ever conceded an approximation of the time. 'Already!' he remarked, amazed. 'Well, let me finish my letter and I'll run out to Moulin Frères.' Renée set off to the storeroom for wine. 'Are we okay for wine?' 'Okay,' confirmed Renée, 'it's just the glasses.' The gallery owner wrote down a few words that seemed wholly unequal to the task of transposing with the requisite tact the subtleties of his current thinking. I'll send the letter tomorrow, he thought, giving up, I'm running out of time. I'm leaving now. 'You can greet the people, I won't be long.' 'And Bruno?' asked Renée with concern. 'When will he be here? I might not be able to handle everyone myself.' 'Bruno,' Alban Wouters conceded, with a gesture conveying his powerlessness on the question of Bruno, 'you know, Bruno and time.'

As Alban Wouters made his way from the gallery, a tram finally pulled out of the terminus at Porte du Midi.

'I don't like being late,' said Simone, who was one of the passengers.

'I told you we should have taken a cab,' said Faya, from the window seat next to her.

'Spoken like someone who isn't paying,' grumbled Simone. Then silence.

They'd been bickering on and off most of the day. Yet the morning had got off to an auspicious start: Faya brought Simone breakfast in bed. 'Sorry, the toast is a little burned,' she apologized, placing the tray on the sheet from which Simone's head and arms poked out. 'I'll be back with coffee,' she said, before clodhopping back down the stairs to the kitchen. Simone rubbed her eyes, then cast her gaze around the room in search of a robe; the one within easiest reach was hanging from the open closet door. Faya was grinding the coffee beans. Simone stepped onto the cold floor, put on the robe, and jumped back into bed as fast as she could, head stuffed under the pillow. She heard the coffee maker whistling for a good minute before Faya, distracted by a magazine or something else perhaps, finally turned off the element, causing the whistling to peter out. Simone heard an 'Oww!'; Faya was congenitally incapable of handling hot drinks without clumsily scalding a finger.

'Coffee is served!' Faya declared as she triumphantly re-entered the bedroom.

'You forgot the butter,' Simone observed.

'The butter!' Faya yelled, already turning around and heading back down to the kitchen before Simone could say, 'It's fine, come here.'

The toast was cold, an observation Simone passed over in silence. Then Faya finally came back with butter and spread it on a slice of toast she bit into with gusto. Crumbs colonized the quilt.

'Are zhou happy, ah leash?' asked Faya, mouth full and eyes wide open.

'Of course!' Simone said, perceiving her own grudging tone but doing nothing to sweeten it.

'Maybe zhou wuh radder eat croi-ahnts?' guessed Faya.

'Right,' Simone mocked. 'Because you would have walked out to the village, in the cold, to get croissants.'

'You're harsh,' said the aggrieved Faya. 'I bring you toast and coffee, and this is how you thank me?'

'Fair enough,' Simone said, 'but who'll pick up all the crumbs?'

'Me, of course,' Faya protested. 'What do you think? C'mon, drink your coffee, it's getting cold.'

'I'm sorry,' Simone said at last. 'I don't know what's up with me this morning. The closing at the gallery, maybe. I never feel comfortable at those things. But that's just how it is. I never know what to say, especially to Alban. He's doing a good job with my drawings. But you have to understand, it all grates on me.'

'*My* drawings!' mocked Faya. '*My* work! It's just Simone Simone Simone around here. And no one ever thinks about poor little Faya. She's forgotten, withering away. Ignored, mocked …'

'Poor little Faya,' Simone shot back, 'spends her days lying around daydreaming, asking for this, demanding that. Poor little Faya only thinks with her –'

'You're mean!' Faya bridled.

'I'm just teasing,' said Simone in self-defence, readying to tuck into another piece of toast.

'Well, I don't like your teasing. Your teasing is mean. And I know what you're all about. Rich family. Born in the right place. Fancy education. You think you can look down on me, just like every bourgeois woman, secure in her privilege. Well, Faya's watching you too. With her wise eyes. Faya doesn't miss a thing.'

'Wise,' Simone said, with sarcasm that did nothing to lighten the mood.

At Moulin Frères, Alban Wouters took his time to pick out wine-glasses with a pleasing roundness and reasonable height, and wondered whether there wasn't something else they needed, before finally settling on paper napkins. Back in his car he had some trouble extricating his vehicle from the iced-over sides of the boulevard, and then tried to avoid a traffic jam by taking an alternate route that proved even more congested. He was more than a little late when he reached the gallery.

Bruno, he was reassured to see, had shown up and was serving wine with that effortless charm he could muster in his sleep. A few visitors were bolting down the canapés the caterer had delivered that afternoon. The gallery owner scanned the room for the artist. He noticed Faya posing, glass in hand, before the drawings of her, moulding her features to enhance the likeness and accepting the compliments of visitors thrilled to converse with such a willing model.

'Simone's not here?' Alban Wouters asked Renée, not without concern.

'Out back, in the alley,' answered the employee. 'Went for a smoke, maybe? We made a sale while you were out. Plus three this afternoon ...'

Alban Wouters approved. Closing nights often brought last-minute sales. But the event was mostly an excuse to throw a little party in the artist's honour, one often less staid than the opening. And now the old familiar faces came trickling in, tugging off hoods and woollen hats and scarves and tracking in clumps of grey snow that it would fall to Bruno to nonchalantly mop up.

In attendance were the splendid Pauline Bogaert, accompanied this evening by the candid Christiane Chorbat, along with the inimitable Kit Polaris, in finery that smacked somehow of the occult, and the lovely Isabeau de Millecieux, dressed as always in black – and in the role of fifth wheel, The Bear, padding around on his great paws, reading each work's label. Faya recognized the crew and set forth in their direction, dispensing kisses and coy hugs. The decibel level kicked up a notch.

'Not bad,' said Isabeau de Millecieux.

'Look,' said Pauline Bogaert, showing her a drawing, 'it's you.'

'And me?' asked Christiane Chorbat. 'Where am I?'

'Who wants wine?' asked The Bear.

'What about Simone? Where is she?' Pauline Bogaert inquired.

'She'll be back,' said Faya. 'And in a real foul mood, I'm warning you.'

'I'll grab a couple glasses at the bar,' said the provident Bear.

'This place has a weird aura,' Kit Polaris said, alluding to something on a wavelength inaccessible to most of us.

'Weird how?' asked Christian Chorbat.

Kit laboured to explain. 'It's everywhere at once, coursing in every direction. The waves are contradictory, that's for sure – but they don't cancel each other out.' Here she closed her eyes and rested a thumb on her temple. 'Quite the contrary, they are growing stronger. As if they were plotting something together. If it weren't the middle of winter, I'd say a storm was brewing.'

'We shall all be struck by thunder!' exclaimed Christiane Chorbat.'

'Pshaw,' said Faya.

At that moment there appeared in the room a tall, upright man, studying the pages of a leather notebook extracted from the pocket of his pelisse. After putting it back in the same pocket, he scrutinized Simone's drawings, one by one, before his eye came to rest on the one entitled *Faya Sitting, 18/20*.

'Thunderstruck indeed,' said Kit Polaris.

As he waited for the red light to turn green, Pierre-Luc massaged the back of his right wrist. The inflammation had returned the day before and, like every other time, he'd let himself sink deep into the dark slough of despond.

His tenosynovitis had made itself felt on Pierre-Luc's thirtieth birthday. At that time he and his studio mates were a hyperactive crew with comics projects everywhere. The diagnosis was shattering: talented though he might be, it turned out that Pierre-Luc had no idea how to hold a pencil. His tendons had paid the price; from that point on he would have to give up everything, lest the damage become permanent. And Pierre-Luc would have fallen into the most total despair that year had not some charitable soul offered him a teaching gig at the art school. Such was his metamorphosis from brilliant young illustrator to dutiful teacher. The new job would prove much less harmful to his sinovial sheath, a region that nevertheless continued to air its grievances, as if bitter at so many years of mistreatment and wholly unmoved by Pierre-Luc's efforts at conciliation, which came too late and amounted to too little.

The light turned green, the rusty station wagon trundled forward. The driver had circumnavigated the block several times without reward, and was in the process of succumbing to the siren song of underground parking. After paying the exorbitant price, he scurried over icy sidewalks toward the gallery.

Simone was finishing off her second smoke when she saw Pierre-Luc at the end of the alley, taking small quick steps and watching his feet. She called out just before he disappeared. He turned around, stupefied at first to hear his name. When he saw who had uttered it, he joined Simone in the alley.

'What's wrong with your hand?' she asked, before he had the time to say something clever.

'My hand? Oh. My tendinitis,' he said dolefully. 'You? Has it started?'

'Yeah, yeah, I was on my way in. Coming?'

'I told my students about the event,' said Pierre-Luc as they went through the gallery's service entrance. 'I don't know if anyone will make it. But there's Sarah-Jeanne Loubier, the one we talked about the other day. She might come.'

Too late, Pierre-Luc: as always, Simone's friends swoop in to steal whatever feeble thunder you have managed to drum up.

'How was it?' queried the one in a vanilla-coloured jacket with ironic crests.

'Sell much?' asked another whose prodigious red mane undulated weightlessly above her.

'It was fine. Sales are good.'

'Did you hurt your hand?' grunted a third voice.

'Tendinitis,' Pierre-Luc murmured, embarrassed that his wrist should be the source of such concern.

'Yeah, it's unpredictable,' said The Bear, pointing at his left paw. 'I had to give up the piano for the same reason. Glass of wine?'

'Sure, thanks,' answered Pierre-Luc distractedly. A subtle gyration of his head brought a previously concealed zone into his visual field, through which he saw Simone being led toward a tall Black man in a pelisse who subtly bowed when introduced to the artist. She met this inclination with a sparkle in the very centre of her eye. Why stop there, fumed Pierre-Luc, go on, kiss her hand while you're at it.

'Red or white?' asked The Bear.

'Red.'

Time passed; Sarah-Jeanne Loubier kept them waiting – had she even remembered?; Simone chatted with her beguiling buyer; Pierre-Luc struggled to contrive an interest in the ambient conversation, including the one foisted on him by that Bear, whose geniality was almost infuriating. Almost.

'You know Simone,' was one of his gambits.

'An honour so many here could claim,' Pierre-Luc shot back.

'The Simone Fan Club,' The Bear rambled on.

'What about you?' parried Pierre-Luc.

'I don't know how long we've known each other,' said The Bear dreamily. 'I wouldn't say I'm a close friend. We see each other once in a while. I do a little work on her house sometimes. What about you?'

'About the same,' Pierre-Luc judged. 'She comes to my drawing class once in a while. The students love her.'

'Oh, wait a minute,' said The Bear with a spark of recognition. 'The drawing teacher. She talks about you all the time.'

This unexpected tidbit should have cheered Pierre-Luc up, convinced him of his significance in Simone's eyes. But no: he saw instead an illustration of the confounding multiplicity of his friend's lives, most of which he had no sense of or part in. To be nothing more than a member, even a member in good standing, of the Simone Fan Club was not what he wanted, was not what Pierre-Luc wanted at all. Jealousy had gotten its paws on him, and he found he was ashamed.

'Excuse me,' said Pierre-Luc to The Bear. 'I'm waiting for someone. I'm going to go see if.'

Back in the main room of the gallery, Pierre-Luc pretended to examine another artist's abstract paintings, displayed in all their pastel blandness. From time to time he shot a look toward the front door, where Sarah-Jeanne Loubier continued to fail to appear. His glass was empty, his wrist a constellation of pins and needles. A little later the tall Black man in the pelisse walked out of the gallery. He was alone, which tempered Pierre-Luc's jealousy, but he carried under his arm a package wrapped in kraft paper that all available evidence suggested must be an acquisition.

A *connoisseur of erotica*, said the narrator of the novel in Pierre-Luc's mind. Italics his.

At this point, one would expect Pierre-Luc to retreat to the back-room to find Simone, where she might still be surrounded by an exuberant throng of admirers. Let's entertain, however, the possibility that, driven by the misplaced pride with which artists have created so many dramas, Pierre-Luc decided instead to mope around on his own until such a point in time as Sarah-Jeanne Loubier should choose to appear.

'We're going to eat,' Simone would say. 'You coming?'

'No, no,' Pierre-Luc would say by way of an excuse, 'I'm waiting for my student.'

'Have it your way,' Simone would counter, masking her surprise.

Pierre-Luc would answer with only an enigmatic nod. And then wait.

Only much later would Sarah-Jeanne Loubier darken the door, eyes half-hidden under bushy chestnut bangs, back bent under a too-heavy bag, looking apologetic to be there at all.

'Oh,' she'd say. 'You're still here. Sorry I'm so late. What happened to your wrist?'

(Insert further explanation of tendinitis.)

'So you're saying you were forced to stop drawing?' Sarah-Jeanne Loubier would exclaim, deeply moved by his account.

'Yeah, but that also made me a teacher,' Pierre-Luc would offer as mitigating circumstances. 'If it weren't for the tendinitis,' he would say, committed to dancing with the story he'd come with, 'I wouldn't have had the good luck' – Would he really say 'luck'? He would – 'to teach you.' And I don't know if I was really good enough to make it as an artist. I was okay, sure ... I think I'm better as a teacher.'

'But we'll never know now,' Sarah-Jeanne would say.

'I could have put out a comic or two,' Pierre-Luc would reckon, 'but I probably would have spent most of my time on illustration contracts. They pay better. Slowly but surely I'd have given up on my own work; best case, maybe I'd be a well-paid freelancer for magazines and kids' books. Just another name in the directory of the illustrators' guild. I'm not saying it's a bad way to go, you know.

A lot of you will end up as illustrators. Only a few will have the kind of career we've dangled out in front of you. It's tough, but that's how it is. And you have to understand that it's better that way, I think, when you have a talent like yours, and good healthy muscles, it's important to push to the very limits of what you can do. Seize every opportunity. Sorry to be so harsh. It's not really my style but it has to be said. We live in a brutal world. Especially the art world.'

After this discussion they'd survey the backroom, which was, after all, the reason for their visit. They'd be the last ones left, aside from the gallery staff, busy cleaning and closing.

'I didn't know she drew that kind of thing,' Sarah-Jeanne Loubier would let slip, and with it the appearance of, what, the seed of some trouble?

In any event, Pierre-Luc would feel, at the sight of Simone's drawings of bodies inflamed with desire and unconscious of their nudity, an ache of his own compounded by his student's uncomfortably close physical presence.

'It is her favourite subject,' he'd eventually spit out. 'Want a glass of wine?'

'White, I guess,' Sarah-Jeanne would say quietly, still intent on Simone's drawings.

'Listen,' Pierre-Luc would say in a commanding tone. 'Go talk to her. She's approachable. You have an exceptional talent, she thinks so, you've already heard it enough from me surely, and she can give you good advice, introduce you to the right people, galleries, art-book publishers, so you'll never have to sell out. There are some things you can't learn from me. See what I mean?'

'You're funny,' Sarah-Jeanne would reply with a serene smile, she who never smiled.

And Pierre-Luc would know he had said too much.

Fabrice Mansaré had been walking with his brown-paper-wrapped package under his arm for a few minutes when a sedan with tinted windows, grey this time, pulled unhurriedly up alongside him. Two thick men got out. One opened the back door. Fabrice Mansaré coolly took his seat next to a small phlegmatic man, different from the last one. The engine started.

'We don't know exactly what you're up to,' said the man, 'nor do we particularly care. We just want you to lie low. For as long as it takes to.'

'I was running some errands,' explained Fabrice Mansaré.

'Sure,' conceded the phlegmatic man. 'Errands. Far be it from us to interfere with your "errands." You're a free man. We're all free men here.'

The man pondered this aperçu at length, like an oenologist according a grand cru the deep and penetrating consideration it deserved. He'd been warned about this Charles Rose. Some said he was a bit of a maverick. But then who wasn't unorthodox, in their field? And was not this unorthodoxy the very hallmark of excellence? The phlegmatic man wondered about Charles Rose's purchase. A work of art. A collector. But the phlegmatic man soon discarded this conclusion, as that epithet had never been applied to Fabrice Mansaré, who, though he might be smiling nervously as he thought of the work laid flat on his knees, secure in its sealed kraft-paper wrapping, was doing so for personal reasons that might well be indelicate to say out loud, but had decidedly nothing to do with his being a *connoisseur of erotica*, as Pierre-Luc insinuated upon watching him leave the gallery.

'I promised to pick this up in person,' Fabrice Mansaré continued, 'and didn't want to break my word.'

'You could have sent someone,' the phlegmatic man argued with a certain cogency. 'We have no shortage of boots on the ground, for "errands" of this kind. Your job,' he stressed, 'is to lie low. And now we'd like to drop you off. Do you have other errands to run on the way?'

The car stopped in a supermarket parking lot. One of the massive men re-emerged half an hour later with a big reusable bag that proclaimed, *I'm green! And you?*

Fabrice Mansaré took the 'green' bag in his free hand.

'How much do I owe you?' he asked.

The phlegmatic man made, for the benefit of all and sundry, an ambivalent gesture conveying both 'The Service will take care of it' and 'Could we please get a move on?'

'Let me assure you,' he said, 'something's in the works. You won't be left twiddling your thumbs long.'

The grey sedan, after reassuming its position in the flow of traffic, took a few aberrant detours, perhaps not strictly necessary since no one was following them, but then there was never any harm in taking such precautions, if for no other reason than to entrench the habit, keep the pencils sharp. So they went for a spin around the Embassy District, wasted entire minutes at three poorly synchronized red lights, slipped under a railway bridge, and drove past a row of more or less abandoned factories before finally making their way back into a downtown draped in fog, past a slow procession of street lamps and galleries, halting in front of the forest of skyscrapers that Fabrice Mansaré was coming to know well. He'd been living there awhile. Night had fallen. Against a backdrop of darkness, hazy halos of light were visible through the car window.

'You can leave me here,' he suggested.

'No,' said the phlegmatic man, 'I insist. We prefer door-to-door delivery.'

At one point in the meal, people believed they heard a muffled detonation, surely from outside somewhere, but not one word was uttered on the subject, and the festivities were not interrupted. Faya wondered what had possessed Simone to invite her wet-blanket drawing teacher friend with the repellent habit of incessantly rubbing his wrists, though she was cheered by the presence of The Bear, who was taking all the man's sadsackery for the team. Simone herself, sitting across from Faya, seemed somehow absent, though the party was in her honour, in a sense, but no, she was off somewhere, forgetful of her barely touched dragon bowl, half-listening to Faya's relentless monologue. It was the kind of day when nothing stuck, connections failed to take, one cast around and tried to fathom the vagaries of life in a vain search for some means to tie the disparate strands into a knot.

The quartet sat in silence around a table for two in a packed vegan restaurant. The Bear, crammed into an unaccommodating corner, had to regularly shift to make way for employees haughtily noting orders on white pads, or carrying soups, salads, and chapati in outstretched, disapproving arms, or tardily dispensing condescending bills. They were lucky to have been seated so quickly: a lineup was now forming in front of the restaurant.

Faya had chosen this uncomfortable eatery – Simone would have opted for the pizzeria now familiar to us, which would have suited Pierre-Luc much better as well. But Faya was determined to cross the street the moment their late supper was finished to a dive-bar-slash-intimate-music-venue called Au Carouge, where already, behind his mixing board, the sound tech was marking levels with a felt pen on the masking tape covering his knobs. The barroom was still empty. The musicians stood waiting for their audience to deign to appear.

On the evening's bill was a group called Poupée Sincère that, Faya had heard, was debuting a new singer freshly arrived in town who had offered her services at the very moment when her predecessor decided, to her bandmates' disappointment, to move to the country and study agronomy. This frontwoman, a stunning blonde of towering stature, had quickly learned the band's list of songs, which were now, thanks to her whisper-like voice, getting a whole new lease on life. She showed up on time for every practice but slipped away right after, spending very little time with the group who, while not holding it against her per se, did have to wonder what sort of future was augured by this aloofness, which in the right light could look almost like contempt. Her sisters in song had chosen to treat their new bandleader like a creature parachuted from another planet.

Pierre-Luc had gone with the flow, from restaurant to bar. He'd paid his cover and offered his still-sore wrist to the doorwoman who had summarily stamped it. He was still regretting not having waited for Sarah-Jeanne Loubier at the gallery, and thus failing to keep what he considered a promise, though in point of fact no promise had been made, and he brooded over his student's (hypothetical) disappointment when she arrived to find him gone – that is, if she eventually made it to the gallery, the devil in Pierre-Luc's ear replied; but she swore she would, the angel countered; and so on and so forth it went as the ancient foes bickered away above Pierre-Luc's head.

The room had filled up. The party settled in at the aluminum bar. Pierre-Luc turned his attention to the generations of silkscreened prints for shows long past on the walls. He liked the faux-tin ceiling.

It didn't take long for Faya and Simone to start bickering over what seemed to Pierre-Luc like a trifle. Perched on an uncomfortable bar stool, The Bear was persisting in his relentless attempts to engage him in conversation; Pierre-Luc, resolved to drown his stabbing pain in alcohol, threw in what he could. He felt strangely at home in this place he was getting to know, and had no problem being half a generation older than the rest of the crowd, as he threw back his G&T and told himself taking a cab home wouldn't be the end of the world.

The first set started, performed by a young man who was also manifestly a shy man, since he was all but hidden behind his collection of laptops and equipment, his absence compensated for by the faded colours of a Super 8 film projected onto his great wall of gear. White waves of sound emerged from the speakers, mostly in the deeper bass frequencies, and in the centre of it all there was a hesitant interplay of rhythms that Pierre-Luc tried to piece together over his neighbours' yammering and cash registers clanking whenever someone bought a drink. Pierre-Luc had always wanted to like musique concrète. He'd never quite managed to wrap his head around any of the recordings he'd tried to listen to, but the style seemed to come into its own here, in situ, with the added layers of the visuals and the cacophony of chatter that seemed not to undermine but rather to uplift the composition. Pierre-Luc was so absorbed in the music he barely noticed Faya and Simone digging in their heels. The only reprieve in their flow of invective came when they chose instead to seethe awhile.

The set ended, and Pierre-Luc filled the intermission with a trip to the bathroom. Around the urinal the white tile was decorated with political slogans and promotional stickers. He took a drawn-out piss and felt like a new man.

Upon his return he found no sign of Simone, just Faya, who turned her back on him. At first he thought Simone had gone to relieve herself as well, but he soon saw that her handbag had also vanished, along with her coat and other accoutrements.

The Bear had disappeared as well, but his things were still there. Most mysterious, thought Pierre-Luc, shrugging his shoulders and turning toward the barkeep, who was simultaneously swamped and in no earthly hurry. Next to Pierre-Luc stood a woman of tremendous height in a black leather jacket whose long blond hair was topped with a backward beige cap. The woman, who seemed to be in the same limbo as Pierre-Luc, waiting for a bartender to notice her, inexplicably turned toward him and flashed a coruscating smile.

Many an author of the male persuasion has waxed lyrical on the staggering power exerted, often unwittingly, by tall blond women, as if this hypothetical society could be viewed as a homogeneous species, entitling us to objectify each member to our ends – a stance that, by the by, would make every individual tall blond woman an iconic paradox, wielding ultimate power over the very desires of men they ever remain accessory to. And yet there simply was something formidably luminous about the woman who that evening graced Pierre-Luc with her smile, an ineffable splendour that partook of the extreme confidence certain people feel in every one of their movements, a purchase she seemed to have over all creation.

'Good crowd,' she ventured in the direction of Pierre-Luc, who would never have dreamed to expect as much.

'I wouldn't know,' answered Pierre-Luc. 'It's my first time here. Is it always like this?'

'It's my first time too.'

'I'm Pierre-Luc.'

'Célestine,' replied the woman, who had finally caught the bartender's eye. 'A big glass of water. The kind with bite.'

'And a gin and tonic,' Pierre-Luc managed to squeeze in, pointing at his empty glass, which the employee flipped upside down on the drain rack where it would wait to be run through the glass washer.

'Are you staying for the next groups?'

'My god!' said Pierre-Luc, pinching himself.

'You won't regret it,' said Célestine with a smile, before slipping off into a crowd whose density had swollen tenfold.

Pierre-Luc swivelled around on his stool again. Faya was gone. What was going on? The background music ceased, the hum of conversation lulled, all eyes turned stageward. A woman whose features led us to infer she had not been born thus had taken to the stage. After introducing herself as MC Blais, she freestyled for a good forty minutes over noise-heavy beats she handled herself. The audience became a crowd; Faya was still nowhere to be seen; the empty bar stools soon filled up, which didn't bother Pierre-Luc, whose sole concern was keeping alive some shred of the elusive Célestine's memory, though he sensed that any hope of reciprocal concern on her part would be foolhardy conjecture. Still, he spent a good part of MC Blais's set lost in dreams of Célestine, and opted for another (dangerously inexpensive) gin and tonic. If Pierre-Luc remained glued to his seat at the bar he would have every chance of crossing paths with Célestine whenever she felt the need for a fresh drink. And indeed a young woman came in his direction and recognized him before he did her.

'Didn't expect to see you here!' exclaimed Sarah-Jeanne Loubier.

'Some friends dragged me,' was the best Pierre-Luc could come up with, pointing vaguely at a hypothetical place in the room.

'Sorry,' Pierre-Luc's student yelled over the din, 'I couldn't make it to the gallery. I had some work to finish. But then I felt like going out. I like this place. Do you know the bands?'

'No,' Pierre-Luc admitted. 'Just checking them out.'

'I came to see Poupée Sincère,' said Sarah-Jeanne, who seemed to glow, as if invigorated by the venue and Pierre-Luc's presence there. 'I heard they have a new singer.'

Pierre-Luc hailed the barkeep, who was becoming quite familiar with her new client. The student, thus solicited, ordered a pint and disappeared.

This night was taking an unusual turn, decided Pierre-Luc, already tormented by feelings of a nature difficult to explain.

As MC Blais's final number ramped up in intensity, finally delivering the long-promised catharsis, the crowd thinned slightly in anticipation of the next act. Faya and The Bear reappeared. Faya looked like she'd been crying.

'Want to sit?' asked Pierre-Luc, perturbed.

'They got in a fight. A bad one,' The Bear explained to Pierre-Luc while Faya made her way toward an empty stool where, once seated, she assertively hailed the bartender.

'I don't understand,' said Pierre-Luc. 'Is Simone gone?'

'I tried to stop her,' said The Bear apologetically. 'She wouldn't listen. She jumped in a taxi and made me promise to look after Faya until tomorrow. It's complicated,' he added.

'I don't get it,' Pierre-Luc said inanely.

'Go, go, go!' said Faya, counting the shooters of tequila she handed out. 'Cheers!' she screeched like a banshee.

The two others did the same. Pierre-Luc choked a little.

'Another round!' said Faya, her hand already raised above the bar.

'What are you going to do?' Pierre-Luc asked The Bear.

'Honestly,' said The Bear, 'I have no idea. My place is tiny. And I don't know, it's really … you know how Faya is.'

'How Faya is,' Pierre-Luc acknowledged.

'One more!' Faya said, returning with two more glasses.

'Damn,' Pierre-Luc assessed, after round two.

'Party!' observed The Bear.

'Not sure how that happened,' Pierre-Luc admitted.

'And how's your wrist?'

'My wrist,' Pierre-Luc continued, contemplating his hand without identifying any cause for concern.

'Ooh la la,' sighed The Bear, who had also moved on to other cares.

'You've got to admit,' said Pierre-Luc, giving his new friend a gentle elbow to the ribs. 'Faya's funny. A great girl.'

'One of a kind,' said The Bear.

'She's got a certain … grace,' said Pierre-Luc.

'Round three!' said Faya, appearing with new drinks for all.

Pierre-Luc choked again.

'Want something else instead?' asked Faya, refreshed.

'Not quite yet,' Pierre-Luc gasped.

'Whatever you want,' said Faya. 'You've got a tab going.'

The crowd was set in motion again and the three friends leaned up against the bar as best they could. On the stage the musicians were assuming their positions: drum, bass guitar, electric guitar. Two Casios stood within reach, stage left. The guitarist hit a couple chords, twiddled a knob on his amp, struck a few more chords. The drummer started in on a basic beat, accenting the offbeat, which the bassist was also hitting, after which it was the turn of the guitarist who, apparently satisfied with the sound, jumped into the mix. At this point the new singer took to the stage and threw Pierre-Luc for a loop. This night was granting no emotional quarter.

'Célestine,' he uttered.

'Gorgeous,' chimed in Faya, startled.

Under ardent spotlights, Célestine soon removed her leather jacket, leaving only a grey hoodie that half-covered a long white T-shirt whose bottom draped over pink cigarette-cut jeans above a pair of white half-leather and half-canvas high-tops. She clenched the mic in a manly grip and started singing in a high-pitched, aspi-rated voice, a flow winnowed to a vaporous stream her tightening larynx would periodically cause to crack, erupting into a keen wail that, just when it seemed poised to slip her control, would come back into key, a sinewy sigh freshly exhaled from a private reservoir of oxygen normally inaccessible, save perhaps for creatures from another world.

—

Pierre-Luc spent the night awash in troubling dreams and woke with a start in a bed of unfamiliar smell and texture. He wasn't immediately convinced he was not still in some dreamland. The room he found himself in was still dark. He felt a stab of pain accompanied by mild nausea – but, surprising mercy, no migraine. He continued to survey his immediate surroundings, discovering pressed up against him the copper-coloured skin of the shoulder blade of Faya, snoring. Several fuzzy questions collided in Pierre-Luc's beleaguered mind and collapsed in a heap from which not one picked itself up. The befuddled plot thickened when Pierre-Luc became aware of the presence, on Faya's other side, of the peacefully slumbering Bear. It was, it must be said, a truly massive bed that could easily have held a fourth.

Pierre-Luc pulled himself from his spot with great care and cast around for his clothes. But no garments were to be found, as one might have expected, in little mounds on the bedroom floor. It was neat as a pin, one might even say suspiciously bare. In any event, Pierre-Luc's bladder left him no choice but to reassess his priorities. He left the room through a slightly open door from which he endeavoured to elicit no creak.

The bathroom was both very large and very new, equipped with Jacuzzi bath and separate shower stall, pedestal sink, and sandstone counter. On the toilet, Pierre-Luc sought to put some order to his ideas. First things first: where was he? He seemed to remember The Bear telling him he lived in an apartment too small to bring a single person back to, let alone two. Nor could he imagine Faya living anywhere quite so chic, that is if she lived, in the sense of making a permanent abode, anywhere at all. They definitely weren't at Simone's. He knew her house; this wasn't it. He harboured furtive thoughts of Sarah-Jeanne Loubier, a hypothesis rejected but not before instilling in Pierre-Luc such a deep shame that the thought could even be entertained. Then he was revisited by the image of naked bodies slumbering in the room next door, a memory that put him in a thoroughly disturbing state of trepidation. He decided to take a shower, which stretched out into twenty full minutes of uninterrupted soaking.

When he ventured out of the bathroom saronged in a towel, Pierre-Luc was privy to a private, hoarse conversation that came not from the bedroom but from another as-yet-unexplored chamber doubling as living room and kitchen. Pierre-Luc went forth and found his two embarrassed-looking friends wrapped in bedsheets on an off-white couch. A tall blond woman appeared in a robe and put two cups down for them on the coffee table. It was Célestine.

'Coffee?' she asked Pierre-Luc, all smiles.

The coffee table held fastidiously stacked pop-music magazines. On one side of the room a high-end stereo played an inscrutable single, electronic. A surprisingly modest record collection was carefully stored behind a glass shelf. The room was free of books.

'Please. Coffee would be great,' said Pierre-Luc at last, after sitting on the armchair across from the couch.

'Well. Quite a night,' said The Bear, to break the ice.

'Quite a night,' Pierre-Luc echoed.

'I wonder,' pursued The Bear, 'how it ended for Simone.'

'Scamp!' Faya exclaimed. 'Swindler! Criminal! Scallywag! She'll miss me to death. Good riddance! I'm taking a shower.'

The Bear and Pierre-Luc watched her stride away, looking unstoppable until she suddenly stopped to kiss Célestine on the lips, then disappeared into the bathroom and vigorously slammed the door.

So Simone was spending her days in a robe before the blazing hearth. What else would you have had her do, freed of her Faya? From time to time she went outside, fetched wood, then fed the fire. And don't think even for a moment that she was pining – she was perfectly content. As you well know, it sometimes happens that we meet someone, one human being in particular who at first glance is of a piece with all the rest but in time sends our internal compass so far out of skew – permit me to run with the first metaphor that springs to mind – that the cardinal north of our compass now appears beyond all doubt to have been untrue from the start, we should instead have pointed our gaze south, or, rather, toward that point that formerly stood in for south while it was all that time our one true north; in any case, you get my point, the magnetism of the poles has undergone an irrevocable shift, as well it must from time to time – we're not against irrevocability per se, as long as it still leaves us room to improvise, as it is only in improvisation that we abandon ourselves fully to euphoria and take the plunge, headlong and naked, loudly proclaiming for all to hear that we just do not give a damn, and accept in the eyes of the world this irrevocable reassignment of magnetic attraction: south not north, or north remapped to south, the world flipped upside down or rather back onto its rightful axis, south and north suddenly made new, dispatched to the tropics for all we know, the old poles now left nameless, barren blocks of ice or of whatever's left. Imagine that meeting a human person had such an effect; it happens; I'm not even going to attempt to marshal the mimetic force required to make you understand: simply imagine that you one day met a human whose being convinced you north was south, south north.

Simone is thinking of Charles Rose – which is to say of Fabrice Mansaré, according to certain information we are privy to, though we cannot vouch for the complete accuracy of our intel, informants being a sly lot.

Simone hadn't merely whiled away a few minutes in conversation with the man with the dazzling smile; no, she'd felt the full force of a magnetic shift that occurred as they spoke, a sudden influx of heat of which only this unknown man could be the cause. And this new acquaintance who went by the name of Charles Rose had made what was, from a buyer, a most astonishing request. That most beautiful of unknown men had spoken thus:

'I'd like you to draw me.'

'Any time,' Simone replied. 'Just come by my studio.'

'It would be best,' answered the stranger, 'if it would not be too inconvenient, if you could come by my house. I'm in an unusual situation. My work,' he said without further elaboration. 'If it's not too much trouble.'

'Not at all,' answered Simone, already pleased at the idea of drawing this charming man who perhaps didn't fully understand what he was asking. 'I don't mind going to your place.'

After which the man bowed before setting off with *Faya Sitting*, 18/20 under his arm, and also, less apparently, on the first empty page of a little leather-bound notebook drawn from the pocket of his pelisse, the phone number of Simone, who had since that day occupied herself with waiting, all alone, surrounded by winter, before a fire it now fell to her alone to tend, not especially nervous but simply eager for the next chapter to finally be written.

(A digression before the next chapter)

'And where's she staying now?' asked Simone when The Bear came by to pick up Faya's things. 'On Célestine's couch,' said The Bear. 'You know Célestine, the singer, Poupée Sincère's new singer?'

'That super-hot tall blonde?'

'The super-hot tall blonde.'

Simone took her temperature. No, not jealous, not jealous at all, not even of a super-hot tall blonde.

CHARLES ROSE

Fabrice Mansaré's daily meditation was rudely interrupted when he sensed the presence of an intruder moving silently through his dark apartment. Undoubtedly out of consideration for the neighbours, the intruder had chosen a knife as his weapon. He tiptoed silently until he was standing behind the man whose unexpected and unsettling nakedness caused him to hesitate a fraction of a second that proved fatal when Fabrice Mansaré pounced, dodged the outstretched blade, and shoved his thumbs into his assailant's carotid artery.

The homicide completed, our hero spent a few moments planning ahead. The intruder's face was wholly unknown to Fabrice Mansaré, just one more guy with peach-coloured skin like so many others. He was annoyed but not surprised to find no identification on the corpse beyond a credit card in a name he imagined to be fictional, or perhaps authentic, if the bearer's name was indeed Poulcq.

Fabrice Mansaré owned a garment bag for which he had yet to find a use. In it he wrapped the interloper, who was beginning to turn white, and then hoisted the heavy weight onto his shoulder and into the back closet where he finally closed the door with a great sigh of relief. The sudden drop in adrenaline levels left him in a state of deep lassitude, and he collapsed onto the chair from which he had so suddenly leapt, as if to plunge back into the terrible daydream from which the intruder had inconsiderately yanked him. In this daydream he could have sworn he remembered a smell, a soap he thought, olive oil or lavender, and skin, of course, the dark skin under that soap.

He had entirely forgotten that he was expecting a visitor that day.

Simone had taken a few steps into the lobby of the rental building and unconsciously scraped her wet boots on a mangy mat that had seen many boots before.

A mild spell had melted the bulk of the snow, sending dirty rivulets running alongside the sidewalk. The tram dropped Simone off at a square in downtown Bruant bordered by shops, an art supply store among them, where she planned to buy a new bristol pad. She hung out in the store awhile, to kill time, and picked up a new mechanical pencil, orange, unlike her other one, which was blue.

As she waited for her appointment with Charles Rose, she felt rusty: drawing Faya had become too comfortable a habit, one she now found it necessary to throw off. And so she'd invited her next-door neighbours over, an adorable couple, sculptors both, to pose for her and help her retrain her hand. They'd started with a few mojitos (in proportions Simone saw to personally, preventively cutting her own with still water). Next she tossed off a few sketches, never spending more than a minute on the head, while mechanically sparking new life into conversations that seemed to grow progressively more animated. The woodstove kept the living room toasty, sonatas tickled the speakers' skins, and Simone, when she judged her guests ripe, took off her old cream-coloured open-knit sweater, under which she had on only a white tank top. It was a signal of sorts, one her guests immediately understood, indeed one they had been waiting for with butterflies in their stomachs, that moment when one might tell oneself, with no risk whatsoever of convincing a soul with the ruse, that it sure was getting hot in here, and begin stripping away all accoutrements. And then Simone would raise her eyes from the sketchbook and take note of her models' nudity, casting away the large sheet on which she had been drawing heads and finding in its stead a new virgin expanse to work on, without hesitating to periodically encourage her subjects to feel free to move around the space a little, the better to explore the art and science of upstroke and downstroke. Then, phrased this time in the form of a suggestion, she'd remind her subjects that they were together in the room: together, naked, and in love. Simone's soothing, neutral voice was somehow self-effacing, instilling in her models the belief that they might actually be alone in the world yet observed at the same time (a paradox more intoxicating than any mojito), and their eyes took on a newfound clarity and intensity, a mimetic excess, an irresistible feeling of being at the centre of a stage.

Not all her models let go with such ease; some were constitutionally unable to let go at all, and Simone had worked hard to learn to recognize this prudish modesty often carefully concealed behind a veneer of bravado because, after all, all anyone ever wanted was to please Simone, to give her the material to make her art, this art of which she seemed to be in such natural and full control that any recalcitrance on the part of her model would have felt like an exercise in insubordination and proof of illegitimacy.

But there were other times when even the best of intentions couldn't prevent things from taking an unexpected turn, perhaps because even the most scrupulously minimal mise en scène forced models to behave like those actors on avant-garde film sets denied the scaffold of a script and suddenly tasked with improvising far beyond the director's aesthetic intentions. So it was that this couple, sculptors both, who had begun by exchanging sweet nothings, started squabbling about something even they no longer remembered. An old couple, Simone reminded herself, an explanation that spoke volumes, though it did nothing to change the fact that the rest of the session was wrecked and no one, even after the passage of this tempest in a teacup, would find their way back to that state of nature that might enable them to unselfconsciously resume their little game. Simone stemmed the tide of disappointment by appearing with blankets for the now clear-eyed participants. She gave them tender kisses, together and then each in turn. 'It's perfect, I know where to find you for next time,' she said, making everyone laugh. Then Simone suggested a new round of mojitos. She didn't water hers down this time.

Days passed, and the awaited phone call finally came. 'Remember me?' Charles Rose asked Simone, his dulcet tones little more than a whisper. Just how clearly she remembered him was something Simone was loath to admit. Nor had he forgotten her. They had both simply waited for the propitious moment when Fabrice Mansaré was free of other obligations. Apart from the attempted assassination, but then who can predict such things?

Charles Rose had been warned his dormancy was drawing to an end. Soon he'd be called into play and assigned a less passive role. Going out was still verboten, so he watched the snow fall from his window, contemplated the enchanting spectacle, a pure fabrication of his adversaries, he thought, seeing as it could only hope to weaken his defences.

The heat was on full blast; he'd taken to spending most of his day in his robe. He wondered whether he wasn't letting himself go a bit. The morning of his appointment with Simone, he'd dusted the shelves of the hi-fi, manoeuvred his vacuum around the apartment, mopped the floor, wiped the surfaces of various appliances. Then he shaved and took a shower. After that he waited, plunged into that unconscious and protracted state he increasingly experienced as a euphoric drug. It was from this very state that he was yanked by an intruder who held his life in low regard. Then, fifteen minutes of torpor. Then the intercom rang, and Fabrice Mansaré was reminded why he had so meticulously cleaned his apartment that day.

Charles Rose greeted Simone in a robe of bluish-grey silk. She was not oblivious to his state of near undress, but kept her feelings to herself and entered the spotless apartment.

There she saw *Faya Sitting, 18/20*, still grounded, leaning against the hallway wall, the sole artwork in the entire place save a children's drawing stuck with a magnet to the fridge. Simone's surprise was even greater to find herself in no wise aggrieved to see her drawing not yet hung on the wall of a living room or bedchamber, a negligence all the more incongruous in these otherwise impeccable surroundings. The austere decor took Simone aback. The opulent neighbourhood and building had led her to imagine the home of a well-heeled collector teeming with works designed to proclaim their owners' superior taste to all comers. Instead, she found herself in a bachelor pad so devoid of any trace of personality that it felt like a model suite. The only clues: a porcelain vase painted with a bouquet of magnolias and buds; a striking chandelier made of three cylinders suspended asymmetrically one atop the other, encrusted in crystals holding court stoically above them: objects that, considered jointly by Simone, were as opaque as any rebus.

The man suggested cocktails. He needed a pick-me-up. The drama of the previous hour had left him shaken. Simone discerned both a certain tension and that she was not its cause. They settled on old-fashioneds; the man apologized that a slice of lemon would have to stand in for the orange, then noticed he was also out of maraschino cherries. At least he had the Angostura bitters. And of course there was the whisky, a single-cask no less, whose quality far outstripped their requirements. Simone wasn't in the habit of taking such strong drink before working, but why not, old-fashioned it would be; they toasted and put one back and the man asked Simone what was next.

'Position yourself somewhere you feel comfortable,' Simone suggested.

'How about right here?'

They were sitting at opposite ends of a modular L-shaped sofa. Simone pulled her materials from a faux-alligator bag and sat cross-legged, ready to work, back leaning against the couch, sketchbook between her thighs. Modular though it may be, sharing couches with models breached Simone's unspoken rule. She wondered whether she ought to be stricter.

The man looked at her with large, placid eyes. Simone met his gaze, but now it was the artist at work directing her eye, just as she directed the hand already outlining on paper the deep black of a face lightened only by sparkling black-irised eyes and a flash of teeth as perfect as a royal flush. The man seemed to take great pleasure in putting himself on display, but the composition of his face, fascinating though it may be, was fixed around that knowing smile whose controlled inscrutability troubled Simone. Only once did he appear to emerge from this detachment, when a look of concern flashed over his face – he must have remembered the dead body in his closet – and Simone was swift enough to capture this reptilian lapse in a portrait that would come back to disconcert her later, in the light of the many secrets regarding her model she was destined to unearth.

'Would you like me to take off my clothes?' the man offered.

Simone fell into a momentary reverie. So many people eager to undress for her.

'If you'd like,' she said. 'If you'd feel comfortable like that. Or you could take it one step at a time. Maybe start by undoing the belt of your robe.'

'Okay,' he said, calmly doing just that.

'Though …' Simone demurred, already at work on a virgin sheet, 'I feel less and less sure of my hands these days, so the folds in the fabric … may not come out quite right.'

'Training,' he answered, elliptically.

'Yes,' she understood, and kept on drawing, 'training, though of course in my line of work we call it practice. I've been a little lazy these past few months. So, out of nowhere like this ...'

'I don't believe a word of it,' he said with a smile.

Simone outlined as best she could the contour of his collarbones, beneath which she could see her model's hairless chest and astonishing abdominals. Who would have expected so much muscle on a frame that had looked so svelte under the pelisse.

'Aren't you full of surprises, Charles.' (She used his first name now, to build the chemistry – an artist's informality, if you will.) Charles Rose looked at her sideways. His arms spread nonchalantly over each arm of the L. The two wings of his robe were parting. He looked strangely relieved, as if unburdened of a secret. His languishing cock bobbed up and down.

'You're the surprising one.'

A memory not readily translatable into words interrupted his train of thought: a kind and very ancient face, a woman, peach-coloured skin. Slender like Simone, and very sweet. This woman, he could still remember, had appeared in his life out of nowhere when he was a teenager, and disappeared just as suddenly. He tried to recall the circumstances.

'Astonishing,' Charles Rose continued, relocating his buttery smile and comestible charm.

Fixated on her drawing, Simone registered the compliment after a delay. At that moment two intelligences cohabited within her: one held the pencil, analyzed space, drew lines; the other had not forgotten a single detail of the upheaval of her initial meeting with this charming man, nor how it had dislodged Faya from her place in Simone's heart. And then, of all the nudes on the gallery wall, it had been toward Faya that Charles Rose's admiration tended. She put her sketchbook down on her knees and contemplated Charles Rose with a doubly haunted look. And he, looking right back at her with an increasing intensity, was moved by the physical proximity of this woman with whom he had so much in common, and whose most intimate design he was surprised to guess and understand. We're monsters, he thought. The world happily tolerates us so long as we keep acting our parts – good thing we're born actors both. Charles Rose momentarily forgot his stratagems. He softly registered his wish.

'Give me your legs.'

If adventure itself could speak, its one true voice would be just so, at once suave and imperative. Simone let herself go, but didn't quite throw caution to the wind.

'Okay, but just one. Left or right?'

'The left.'

Simone stretched her left leg toward Charles Rose. He delicately removed her sock and in the same motion caressed her undercalf; then his hand landed on her foot, and to the very shallowest part of the arch he deliciously applied his thumbs.

'Whatever you're doing, don't stop,' Simone ordered.

The epilogue to this scene spread out over several days. Each discovered a penchant for the other, one better consummated sooner than later. Sucking their pleasure to the marrow, they no sooner reached a climax than the time came to begin afresh. Joyful was the discovery of their shared antipathy for base copulation, an act that procured at best only middling pleasure and to which both preferred more elaborate proceedings. With boundless skill she stroked him off with one hand while the other eased her pocket vibrator into the narthex of his anus. He performed such masterful cunnilungus she could have sworn it was a woman's work. Their games often veered toward this swapping of roles, along with a full battery of metaphors from the world of pastry: a breast became a cream puff, a stomach a *noix charentaise*; the vulva was a mille feuille, the clitoris a meringue; toes were transfigured as salambo, bottoms a shortbread, the cock a chocolate éclair – delicacies they then had delivered at exorbitant expense, to figuratively consume the beloved body and then, in a carbohydrated daze, leap right back into heinous new debaucheries.

After a few days on this high-calorie diet, they decided to wed.

There remained the outstanding matter of the corpse.

And that's where we came into play – 'we' meaning my associate, Debruyn, and myself. The Service informed us that Charles Rose had encountered a minor logistical hitch. As usual, Debruyn left the questions to me. Charles Rose hadn't identified his attacker. At any rate, the first order of business was to clear out the closet, where the smell was getting funky. There were neighbours to consider. And of course there was no need to get the local uniforms involved in a matter that was at best of tangential concern to them, and of which they'd understand, let's not mince words, squat. The Service was of the opinion that we knew all we needed to know. Debruyn pointed toward the door.

We both enjoy jobs that end with us tossing a body of flesh into a body of water: there's a satisfying symmetry, an almost poetic sense of closure. It always reminds me of the stories that my dad, a navy man, used to tell. I reached into my old dad's trove, as is my wont from time to time, for a yarn I was sure Debruyn hadn't yet heard, while he was busy scoping out the cars parked along the Old Port Road, a byway lit only intermittently by the odd street lamp and unfrequented at this hour when north winds blown in by a stormy sea were not amenable to evening strolls. I was sharing my meteorological observations with Debruyn when an Anderloni coupe caught his eye, likely on account of its curves but possibly also for its vibrant colour; he proceeded to expertly pick the lock, with an occasional port or starboard glance.

In the yellow coupe we made our way downtown. I turned on the car stereo as a courtesy to Debruyn, who had inquired whether it would kill me to shut my goddamn trap for five measly minutes, just this once. He then, inexplicably, tuned the radio to a call-in show. By my timepiece we were slightly early for our rendezvous.

Charles Rose's building had underground parking. Down we went, as if nothing could be more natural, with a little wave at the attendant bravely pretending not to nap, then tucked the Anderloni away in a corner, behind a concrete pillar next to the elevator. Debruyn turned off the engine, and with it the car stereo, and we waited for Charles Rose to appear.

At the appointed time he emerged from the elevator with a large and malodorous bundle slung over his shoulder. While pickup service doesn't fall outside our job description, he'd insisted on basement drop-off because he wasn't alone, or so he'd led us to believe. We inferred he was in the midst of an amorous encounter, certainly none of our concern. Charles Rose seemed tense but relieved to be rid of the body. While relief at our presence was understandable, I picked up also on a strange embarrassment, an amateurish qualm, and deduced that Charles Rose was not in the habit of killing.

These were the halcyon days before security cameras colonized every nook and cranny. Good thing too, as no small amount of flapping around was required to stuff our stiff into his final conveyance. One constant of our missions was Debruyn's infuriating tendency to swipe vehicles that combined an unimpeachable sense of style with a patent deficiency in cubic footage, a matter I was disinclined to bring to his attention.

Our cargo eventually agreed to being stuffed into the back, and we bade adieu to our client, who didn't seem inclined to spend a moment longer than was strictly necessary away from his apartment. The guard whose slumber we had interrupted conscientiously raised the gate and we headed west, hurtling down Haucourt Drive and into the black night.

There, tucked in among the warehouses in a cheerless alley in a district now frequented exclusively by cutpurses and ne'er-do-wells, we found a long-abandoned service station whose garage door was no match for our lock pick. Inside, waiting faithfully as a car at a stop sign, was our trusty Cholet Model 7B. Debruyn got busy anonymizing the corpse on a rough-hewn work table still cluttered with old bottles of motor oil and antifreeze. The humid late-winter air chilled us to the bone, and I suggested Debruyn might wish to pick up the pace, to which he countered that I might contrive to give him a hand for once in my goddamn life instead of prattling on pointlessly, an argument whose merit I was hard-pressed to deny. I took the opportunity to peruse our specimen's wan face.

'How about that,' I said. 'It's Poulcq.'

'Yep, looks like old Poulcq all right,' Debruyn confirmed.

Now what the hell was Poulcq doing at Charles Rose's apartment?

We flipped a coin; I got to drive the yellow Anderloni to the deserted Ostden Bluffs. On the radio the talk turned to the peccadillos of Prince Ludwig, and though I'm a republican at heart, I couldn't help but be riveted by the sordid domestic dramas that seem to be the exclusive purview of heads weighted down by crowns.

The morning sun was rising when Debruyn drove up to meet me in the Cholet. The yellow coupe took a dive, bearing its final passenger into the cold, choppy sea beneath.

A person drawing knows the shapes of things but not their name. Names, after all, would only be a burden, inhibit the work, stay the hand. And drawing must be without inhibition; a drawing needs to move untrammelled and to be free to run away. The Porte du Midi district teemed with human figures strolling, each at their own pace and with their own distinctive gait. The main thing was not to obsess over (or take naive amazement in) this particularity, but rather to behold each one for what it was, temporarily extricating them from the flow of the reality whose essence they formed, and to use the bristol paper as a means of transport; take them for a stroll with the point of your pencil; keep just the smallest trace, unbeknownst to them, immortalized on paper, here on the still-chilly café patio where Simone sat lurking. Once relinquished, these human forms remained mysterious as ever, released back into the flow of the real to pursue their inscrutable forward march over the cobblestones of a historic district still irrigated by the winter's snows.

A student whose look of perpetual amazement from time to time shone through her hedge of bangs approached the table where Simone sat drawing. 'Hello,' she ventured, 'remember me?' Simone, deep in that place where she'd lost her grasp on the names of things, hesitated a moment before finally answering. 'Mademoiselle Loubier. Of course I remember. Have a seat. Are you in a rush? Do you have a minute? For coffee. I'll call the waiter over.'

Sarah-Jeanne Loubier sat down, sketchbook set studiously on her knee. The patio was empty. It wasn't quite the season.

'It's a good place for observation drawing,' noted Sarah-Jeanne.

'I was in the neighbourhood, with time to kill,' Simone admitted. 'And I'm getting rusty, so rusty,' she said, with a glance at her last sketches. 'Drawing is an unforgiving mistress. The second you stop, the work suffers. You have to draw constantly, all the time, every moment of every day.'

The waiter appeared. Sarah-Jeanne ordered a bowl of café au lait, Simone a second espresso.

'Sorry, I'm not here to teach you a lesson.'

'Well, actually … if you want,' countered the surprised student.

'Show me what you've got,' said Simone, pointing at the sketchbook.

Sarah-Jeanne Loubier complied. Timidity be damned, she had to continue along this new road she had set down, the road that led her to Simone, whom she had happened to catch sight of, drawing away on this abandoned patio in the Porte du Midi.

'That's all well and good,' said the master. 'But all over the shop.'

'Really?' answered the apprentice.

'I won't beat around the bush,' said Simone after a drawn-out pause. 'You're mad talented. You've really got the touch. And style, more than I'll ever have. But you still have a lot to learn. Look at this one. We can see where you hesitated. And it's pretty obvious that you gave up at one point. Look at those folds. You backed down, it's lost. Whereas here you didn't know when to leave well enough alone. Your last good line, the last true line, was this one. After that you take off in every direction at once. As if you didn't want to admit that sometimes a good drawing requires very little from us. You've got a strong sense of composition, mostly. This is awkward, though. Toss it.'

The coffee showed up. Sarah-Jeanne, in shock, didn't dare touch hers. Simone, busy flipping through the young woman's sketchbook, also ignored her espresso.

'Okay, I get it,' she went on. 'This sketchbook has everything you've ever done.'

'Well …' Sarah-Jeanne hiccupped.

'Let me explain something,' Simone said gently. 'When you take your portfolio to show, I don't know, say Alban Wouters,' she added with a winking smile. 'Alban isn't lazy, exactly. He's got nothing against a thick portfolio. But he's looking for an artist who can read her own work, cull it into a coherent whole …'

Simone saw in her companion's look the shame that follows a serious faux pas. Am I cruel to talk to her like this? she wondered. Simone decided not to add to Sarah-Jeanne's embarrassment by dwelling on it. Instead, she opened the sketchbook again, pulled out a selection of drawings made with pencil crayons, and looked them over with apparent admiration.

'See, here now, you've got something like a series. Same technique, similar subjects. We'd need to pick and choose. There are a few weaker ones. But if we keep the best of the lot, we'll have a presentable series. I think Alban might be interested.'

'Really?' said Sarah-Jeanne, moved.

'You know what? I have to be on Boulevard des Anciennes Colonies in fifteen minutes. But. Why don't you stop by my house this week. With your sketchbook. Bring everything, if you want. We'll look through it all together. I'll help you put together your portfolio. Then we'll get you a meeting with Alban.'

Sarah-Jeanne thanked her effusively, swore eternal gratitude. Simone assured her it was nothing, her one wish was to help Sarah-Jeanne make her way. She paid the bill and squeezed between the patio tables after bidding the young woman a final goodbye. After all, she thought, no one ever took me under their wing, or helped me put together a portfolio. Simone's career had taken off on its own, fuelled by good luck and libertinage, but this devil-may-care approach had sometimes taken a heavy toll. It was only right that she should help this young woman find her way, she thought, congratulating herself.

The Boulevard des Anciennes Colonies (formerly Boulevard des Colonies) was a major high street with wide sidewalks under the signs of large department stores. Protected by a violet coat against the chilly air that carried a whiff of the sea, Simone weaved between pedestrians toting rectangular bags. She met the eyes of the people she passed on the street, by turns jealous and infatuated, swollen with unanticipated desire she was surprised to discover herself the source of. *I'm in love,* she realized. It's clear for all to see. My every movement betrays the fact that I've made love a thousand times in the last week.

Without warning, she turned into a small street that forked again at a right angle three hundred metres up. She pushed open the door and climbed two flights of stairs. Someone admitted her to an old office piled high with rare books.

'Oh, my dear, dear friend!' said old Arthur Hazel, kissing Simone on either cheek. 'Again we're honoured with your presence!'

A tall woman appeared, of a certain age and authoritative presence, wearing a skirt cut from the same fabric as her flamboyant turban, a yellow-patterned Faso Dan Fani. A line of kohl intensified a gaze already hard to hold.

'Simone!' she exclaimed, taking her in her arms. 'My little Simone!'

'What are you doing here, Mom?' asked Simone with a touch of snark she couldn't quite hide.

'Oh, I was in the neighbourhood,' said her mother evasively. 'And Arthur mentioned that you had a meeting. So I thought I'd drop by. Aren't you happy to see me?'

'Of course. It's not that,' Simone lied.

'And what is this I hear? You're getting married? To a new man?'

Simone wondered whether the object of her mother's concern was marriage in general, or marriage to a man in particular.

'That'll be your fourth!' (It would, in effect, be Simone's fourth.) 'Imagine that, Arthur. My daughter's already been divorced three times. And here she goes trying again! Just have kids already!'

'Mom!' Simone yelled. 'I'm fifty!' (Also accurate, within a year.)

'Well, you don't look it!' Arthur Hazel assured her.

Madame Bilitis Bergmann, for whom any conversation of age served only to remind her of her own, grew dispirited.

Old Arthur Hazel, perhaps to change the subject, took an antique volume down from the shelf.

'Have I already shown you this remarkable treatise on botany? Several hundred years old.'

After examining four or five of the bookman's specimens, Bilitis Bergmann grew bored and invoked a younger brother, that was right, she'd promised to meet him, had to be there in an hour. She kissed her daughter like a woman scorned and promised Arthur, who unctuously escorted her to the door, that she would stop by again soon, et cetera et cetera.

'Now let's look at those proofs, shall we?' said Arthur Hazel when he reappeared.

The publisher opened a folder. A half-title in the top right corner of the almost square page was set with an elegant tightness in a lowercase roman: 'ballerina porteña.' Simone turned the page. The same title reappeared, larger yet still free of the tyranny of the uppercase, followed by 'and other drawings.' At the very bottom was Simone's first name and the mark of her publisher, Hazel-Marchand, the silhouette of a flowering branch of *Corylus colurna* encircled in a thin line. A small nude by Simone occupied the centre of the page, framed by enough white space to let the composition breathe. Simone flipped over this page as well. She relaxed. The printer had done lovely work.

The book opened with a short preface Arthur Hazel had commissioned from a poet friend. Simone lingered on the typographic composition: stretched-out, irregularly shaped italics with ligatures and subtle grace notes, arranged in a single column that covered just a touch more than the left half of the page. She pointed out a typo, which the publisher promptly circled in red pen. With a final glance at the whole, she turned another page.

Abovementioned paratextual apparatus excepted, the book consisted of a series of Simone's drawings, each on its own page, since this was a luxury edition (on Japanese paper, as old Arthur Hazel was powerless to resist indulging Simone's every wish). It opened with the lovely eponymous ballerina of Buenos Aires pulling a stocking off her right calf with an inattentive finger. Some fifteen drawings recorded Simone's time backstage at the Alley Cat Theatre, a venerable institution where she had with joy explored the labyrinthine wings and warrens. This opening series was followed by others, some of which had been shown recently at Alban Wouters's gallery.

To each image its accompanying legend, still scrupulously lower-cased, at the bottom of the page. Simone turned more pages. She saw *Faya, Sitting*. Simone thought a moment. 'Let's begin the series of nudes with this one,' she instructed the publisher, who recorded this reordering along with the other adjustments in his instructions to the printer. Simone got to the end of the book: blank page, motto, colophon, final appearance of the *Corylus colurna*.

Few people could match Simone's passion for reviewing proofs. She personally selected typefaces, vetoed layouts, signed off on the choice of paper. Readers didn't suspect a thing, accustomed as they were to the impeccable publishing standards of the Hazel-Marchand dynasty, but the free, ostensibly spontaneous style of Simone's publications was dictated by their author's meticulous decrees. I missed my true calling, she thought. I should have been a publisher.

The sight of her aged yet spry publisher belied these fatalistic thoughts. No, nothing is lost. I still have my whole life ahead of me.

In the back seat the small phlegmatic man – who was admittedly less so than his two predecessors – was silently running the new information Fabrice Mansaré had provided through the assembly line of his intellect.

'A capital initiative,' he finally admitted as the sedan, blue this time, accelerated with the eagerness of one delivered from a traffic jam. Fabrice Mansaré, to his right, was surprised by this reply.

'The heart wants what the heart wants,' said the phlegmatic man. 'You may be dwelling on how your planned marriage might complicate our plans. But you forget, it also introduces a new element of confusion. And we have no more powerful weapon in our arsenal than confusion. We've already mentioned that your dormancy is coming to an end. You're going back to work. It's come to our attention that Problem 30 is in town.'

'Problem 30,' Fabrice Mansaré repeated. He'd heard enough to know the Service was extremely wary of the Melanco operative who used that moniker.

The sedan had pulled onto the Périphérique. It was smooth sailing at this time of day. The car was driving fast.

A little too fast.

The small man who was proving to be decidedly less phlegmatic than his two predecessors was looking for something in his briefcase. He found an envelope and held it out to Fabrice Mansaré.

'This is for you. Bring a plus-one. The embassy's holding an intimate reception for Prince Ludwig. You'll attend with your fiancée. Buy her a ball gown. And keep receipts; you have no idea the amount of red tape our friends in Accounting throw our way.'

The sedan weaved jerkily around the car in front of it, narrowly avoiding a second vehicle, then veered just as abruptly into the left lane.

'The brakes have stopped working,' the goon in the front seat diagnosed.

'Pull onto the shoulder,' the phlegmatic man ordered. 'Then turn off the engine and yank on the handbrake. Everyone buckled up?'

'We'll have to find a way to get there,' said Fabrice Mansaré, observing the suddenly packed right lane.

'Oh, we'll get there,' the phlegmatic man reassured him. 'Philippe's an excellent driver. I believe he did a little racing in his younger days.'

'Rallycross,' the right-hand man specified proudly. 'Fourth place, Foulay-Quersac race. Third Division.'

'Still,' said the phlegmatic man, 'it's inconvenient when your brakes give out like that. And peculiar. Above all, peculiar.'

'Clearly sabotage,' confirmed right-hand man number two, who was keeping a close eye on the right lane. 'Now! There's a break.'

'I guess I'm the one they're after,' said Fabrice Mansaré. 'Sorry for the inconvenience.'

'Not at all,' answered the phlegmatic man. 'And what do we know, really. It's not like we don't have enemies of our own.'

'We're going to brake,' the driver warned them.

The tires of the blue sedan striped the shoulder with degraded rubber.

Poupée Sincère's jam space was a nearly cubical room wallpapered with egg cartons where the band's instruments, especially the cumbersome drum set, lived when not needed elsewhere. Two deadbolts had to be coaxed open before the banged-up door would budge. A long dusty hallway led to the practice space and the twenty others that had been rented to bands since the shoe factory that formerly provided the building's vocation had moved and the edifice had joined its neighbours as a portside relic, one of a clutch of hangers-on whose forlorn facades had so far kept the speculators at bay. The idle train tracks now carved paths through baneberry and columbine that turned muddy in foul weather.

Célestine leapt confidently over treacherous puddles, as if alerted to their presence by onboard sonar; Faya did her best to follow.

Faya was a changed woman: petulance had given way to a perpetual state of wonder. She never left Célestine's side. While Poupée Sincère practiced, Faya sat guard on an old couch picked up god-knows-where and upholstered in a vaguely green fabric. With vacant eyes, she watched the group rehearse, for the third time, the verse to 'Facing North,' whose words she'd learned by heart.

> Whalesong whistling o'er the brine,
> I count the buttons on your sleeve.
> Hopes betrayed, hopes deceived,
> When will your secret code be mine?

For some time Célestine had been trying to convince the group to leave their old repertoire behind; she brought new songs, including several of her own. The three musicians agreed that there was something curiously catchy about these new songs and were working to flesh them out with sparkling arrangements whose complexity drove them to practise more assiduously than before.

Time was short: Célestine had booked studio time next week. She was adamant that they record a single ASAP, before summer; everyone knew summer was when bands either broke through or faded away. They laid into 'Facing North' one more time:

Facing north, I play dead,
But the sea knows my true heart.
Facing north I lose my head,
Drown in you, my body my art.

Musical sparks enlivened the melancholy surface of the somewhat hazy succession of images. A funny subject for a summer jam, thought Faya, who was nevertheless powerless to resist this melody that so delicately straddled bitter and sweet. She approached it not as the work of her flesh-and-blood lover but rather like something handed down by those immortals who stare at us from the walls of the best record stores, cryptic expressions on their wild faces. In the centre of the room Célestine delivered her libretto with a concentration so fierce it infected her bandmates, each of whom leaned over their instruments with total application. The impetuous blonde had them all under her sway.

Simone's entrance on Charles Rose's arm caused a stir on the mezzanine. For what could approach the boredom of these diplomatic evenings? In burst Simone in a solar-yellow dress, like a tropical storm in this sanctum of stuffed shirts and gowns. And that tattoo! Oh, that exquisite tattoo between her shoulder blades, a red-splattered pattern fearlessly crossing the border of her dress, like tribal warpaint. And what could possibly be said of her gentleman companion, that tall Black man surveying the scene with those commanding eyes! Such things were seen at the embassy from time to time, it's true. But one also sensed that this particular thing was something altogether different.

Princess Cécile, fresh from a symposium and accompanied by her lover *du moment*, joined the crowd. With a discreet motion she pointed toward the current object of gossip.

'Did you see that hairstyle?' murmured the Countess de Rzewuska.

After a few moments studying the tableau before her, Princess Cécile spoke. 'A breath of fresh air! Clearly an admirable character.'

The court fell into rank around this view; none had so much as entertained thoughts to the contrary. But who knew the name of this sparkling new socialite? For she was of high birth, that much was plain to see.

From the moment he walked in the door, Fabrice Mansaré was wanted elsewhere.

'I'll need to borrow him a moment,' a man in formal attire with bags under his eyes apologized to Simone. 'You must understand, the ambassador is asking personally,' he said, before spiriting the gentleman away from his lady through an unmarked door.

Simone was immediately comandeered by an elderly couple named Grogniard: Bernardine-Isaure and her husband, the professor, an inventor.

'So you're an artist,' said the woman. 'Fascinating! Did you hear that, Albert?'

'An artist. But of course,' the professor observed.

'And naturally you must have a show somewhere?'

'Well,' Simone hesitated.

'A painter, unquestionably a painter. I am of course a great admirer of painting – such an untamed, noble art! It's a travesty that it is held in such low regard today. It's true that one can no longer hope to actually *understand* much of it, with all the scribblers and daubers on the scene. It pains me to say it, but we're losing our values! Or perhaps I'm an incurable nostalgic. We are of course great visitors of museums, isn't that so, Albert?'

'Museums,' adjudged the professor.

'Because man cannot live on science alone!' expounded the grand dame. 'Man must have Art, is it not so, Albert? Man must have Art – wasn't that exactly the point today's speaker was making, this very afternoon, at the Hotel Marie-Clarisse – you should have heard him, whatever was his name again? Was that not indeed the title of his talk? "Man Must Have Art."'

'And perhaps even Woman?' Simone ventured.

'You can say that again,' whispered Bernardine-Isaure Grogniard. 'Just between you and me, I've always doubted whether the word *man* could ever be entirely neutral. If it might not, in fact, be a way to exclude, if you will, our fair sex.'

'It's been said before,' Simone agreed.

That was the moment chosen by a willowy man with a winsome smile to butt into the conversation.

'Forgive my interruption, mademoiselle,' he interrupted. 'May I have the honour of introducing you to an individual who ardently wishes to make your acquaintance?'

So caught off guard was Simone by this *mademoiselle* that it took a while to remember that her hand was free of rings, the type of detail sure not to go unremarked in her present company.

'I beg your pardon,' Simone begged of the Grogniards.

'The brazen charms of the artistic temperament,' cooed Madame Grogniard. 'And kudos on your great work!'

'Indeed,' uttered the professor, jogged from his reverie. 'Best of luck for your next concert.'

'She's a *painter*,' the professor's wife hissed.

Simone was already elsewhere.

'Where did you say you were from, *chère mademoiselle?*' asked the inquisitive gentleman, snapping his fingers at a servant. 'Not around here, at any rate.'

'Oh, but I am. I've lived in Bruant my whole life,' Simone corrected, attempting to conceal her irritation behind a mask of politeness.

'So how is it we've never met? You clearly travel in the right circles. Let me guess: daughter of a good family. Perhaps a large industrial concern …'

'My father is a Bergmann,' she admitted.

'On your mother's side then,' the gentleman hazarded.

'You had someone to introduce me to?'

'Someone,' the man confessed, 'intent on rescuing you from the clutches of that insufferable Grogniard. But let me introduce myself: Émilien Surville, at your service. I hope I may be of some use, and perhaps even some pleasure. Let me cut to the chase: you intrigue me! And you clearly have interesting acquaintances. Tonight it has fallen to you to play the ingenue. You're the one all eyes will turn to, sooner or later.'

'And you?' Simone sallied, surveying the room for any sign of her fiancé. 'What's your role in all this?'

'Mademoiselle, such bluntness will never do here. You won't last five minutes in this vipers' den. I believe,' he chuckled, 'I caught you just in time.'

The man known as Surville was ushering her from one end of the grand hall to the other, in time to the syrupy bolero being phoned in by some languishing band hidden from view.

'I'll tell you everything I know,' he repeated, 'everything there is to be learned – and some things that aren't. You'll make acquaintances of every rank here, and you must learn to distinguish people of consequence from those without significance: the minister from the captain of industry, the duchess from the starlet. And on that matter, do tell me a little something about your gentleman consort.'

Simone felt a surge of desires, not entirely non-violent, which she quelled as best she could because she didn't want an incident. She told the man Charles Rose's name, but was soon struck by the fact that she knew precious little of her fiancé's activities, if by little we mean nothing. Simone had an idea.

'Monsieur Surville, I'm afraid I'm not in a position to speak about who we really are. You understand, surely, in our business …'

She then confidently fastened the imaginary zipper over her mouth. Émilien Surville stopped talking for a moment, taken aback. The pause was long enough for a new person to infiltrate their duo with the clear intent of again spiriting away the newcomer. Surville changed his tune the moment he realized it was Princess Cécile.

'Your Highness,' he said, bowing, 'please permit me to introduce this charming individual.'

At that moment, the three of them stood at the foot of a large granite staircase leading to the mezzanine. The band made busy smothering an ostendaise in a thick coating of syrup.

Princess Cécile smiled in satisfaction as the interloper scurried away.

'So sorry to leave you in the clutches of that deplorable man,' she said. 'Please keep me company instead. I gather you're an artist.'

They walked up to the mezzanine. Princess Cécile, for all her extravagant elocution, had difficulty concealing – made no attempt to conceal, really – an impulsive soul that betrayed her relative youth. She had been thrust into society at a tender age through an advantageous marriage to a prince who had the virtue of being not overly geriatric and the flaw of being reliably inconstant. The socialite's life had given the princess a prosaic view of the ways of the world, one that had begun to tarnish certain aspects of her nature. A sclerotic sadness now underlay her ever-present smile.

This streak of sullen envy was common to the women woolgathering in the vicinity of the princess: ladies of the court, Simone figured, or minor monarchs, chattering away, pretending not to eavesdrop.

Simone began wondering whether Émilien Surville might not be the lesser evil, after all. And wherever could Charles be? She decided to venture a straight answer.

'I make drawings.'

'Fashion?'

'Erotic.'

'Oh!'

A giggle.

Snickering from the hangers-on.

'Are you shocked?'

'Au contraire, ma chère. You mustn't imagine we society ladies are innocents. You know as well as I, our fair sex has an understanding, much more complex than that of our lovers, of the pleasures of the flesh. Sweet affliction at the service of Venus ... But come. I must hear everything!'

In a tête-a-tête on the mezzanine, the ladies had no way of knowing that on the ballroom floor below quite a commotion was brewing.

Debruyn and I had been called in to lend the embassy's welcome squad a hand. It wasn't a disinterested favour. After going through the motions of checking a few guests' credentials, we slipped off toward the ballroom.

Seeing Charles Rose dragged off into the wings had definitely piqued my curiosity. I followed, pushing through the unmarked service door, armed with a tray a member of the serving staff had generously, if not knowingly, procured for me. At the back of the hallway I saw Charles Rose deep in political discussion, and I felt the need to freshen up my disguise. As luck would have it, a new door lay open to the right. I went through.

I immediately noted that the small parlour where I found myself opened onto a second parlour, and then a third, and so on and so forth. After a moment of silent kudos to the architect behind this felicitous disposition of space, I walked on, from parlour to parlour, in a direction parallel to that taken by my client. No sooner had I reached the fourth of these communicating chambers than I made the unwelcome acquaintance of a young buck in a headset who had affixed a contact microphone to the door between him and his coveted conversation. Charles Rose was evidently a person of great interest to the secret service.

It was no great feat to sneak up on such an indiscreet man, absorbed in his headphones, with his back to me. I wanted to remind this oaf that listening in at doors is bad manners, but he didn't leave me much time: my lesson was met with the acute angle of an elbow forcing entry into the domicile of my solar plexus. This sudden turn of events caught me off guard, since I'm easily amused and in the habit of marvelling at even the most hackneyed development in any plot; if it weren't for me and my kind, the entire entertainment industry would go belly up in no time. First things first, I had to get my wits back about me, on the double. The blackguard and his hastily packed-up recording studio were already flying the coop.

Our little game was making a din that was interfering with my perennial love of a job well done. By the time I lithely rejoined our runaway in the nether regions of the vestibule, my movements were thwarted anew, this time by a permanent member of the embassy staff, of imposing bulk, who was persuasive in his efforts to accompany me to the building's entrance, accurately intuiting that my name would be found neither on the evening's guest list nor in any staff directory. None of this solicitous concern for my status was directed toward our fleeing friend, who seemed to enjoy free run of the house, which he was using to make merry with the legitimate guests. The band launched into what may be the least caffeinated Java it has ever been my ill fortune to give ear to. The intruder looked poised to escape.

Debruyn, who had till then remained an anonymous face in the crowd of attendants, now also pierced the celebration's inner sanctum, bumping into the prince consort and a maharajah's wife along the way, and endeavouring with a defensive parry to curtail the intruder's movements. To an accompaniment of vigorous and repeated shoving, he asked the usual questions: 'Who do you work for? What are you doing here?' And so on and so forth. The embassy staff showed no love for my colleague's rough-and-ready ways, and the three of us were soon tossed out like filth into the street, where we might have finally enjoyed a moment to speak freely and easily, had not our John Doe taken advantage of the fracas to snag a taxi that appeared just a little too conveniently, and suspiciously alone. We gave chase on foot a few minutes before admitting defeat: chalk up one more win for machine over nature.

Debruyn and I compared notes. We had made rather too indelible an impression to try going back to the embassy. Debruyn had gathered no information from the party of interest, save for our mark's outburst – 'Nothing! You'll get nothing from me!' – which was proving as prophetic as it had been categorical.

'At least we have that to take back to the Service,' I said soothingly. Debruyn grumbled something as he pressed the button that opened the cassette tray. 'Empty,' he whined. 'To think I was right there,' I moaned, recounting for the benefit of my companion the finer points of my valiant exploits, going into each minute detail of a deployment that unfolded by the book, save for a few strokes of bad luck.

'What is this Charles Rose character up to?' I wondered out loud, while we pounded the lonely wet pavement of the Embassy District. Debruyn found the Cholet, whose drizzle-spattered windshield bore a shameful notice of infraction. There was no parking in the Embassy District, at any time.

The ambassador had accompanied Charles Rose back to the ball-room. His affable face slightly softened the firmness of his speech. Charles Rose expressed agreement with a series of commonplaces.

'We cannot have the minister lose patience,' stressed the ambassador. 'So we must know the general's intentions immediately. I don't need to remind you that the stability of the region is at stake. You can surely see that we can wait only so long. No matter how patient we'd like to be. After a certain point we can no longer guarantee the support in principle we've provided up to now.'

The two men shook hands.

'I'll wait to hear from you.'

Charles Rose took his leave, not without relief. He climbed the granite staircase. There amid a battalion of magpies was Simone, chatting with Princess Cécile as if they were old friends. She doesn't waste a minute, he thought, impressed. Simone's face then turned amorously toward his, and the circle parted, as if by magic. The musicians were endeavouring to soldier through at least a basic waltz.

Charles Rose took Simone's hand, and the soon-to-be-weds went down the staircase, with pomp and circumstance, under the gaze of an emotional princess; still without taking their eyes from each other, they advanced to the centre of the hall where a space opened to make way for the couple. Simone remembered the steps; it had been a while, but everything was still in there somewhere. Charles Rose moved like someone who dances every day of his life.

'Is everything okay?' asked Simone softly.

'Work,' her fiancé answered. 'Nothing to write home about. Looks like you made some new friends.'

'New friends?'

'Princess Cécile,' Charles laughed, 'isn't the type to show interest in every new face she sees.'

'Good god, poor princess!'

'Perhaps I'm being indiscreet,' admitted Charles Rose.

'Her husband is neglecting her.'

'Oh?'

'As is her lover.'

'Hm.'

'She doesn't know her way around the city.'

'Ah.'

'And she'd love nothing more than to go shopping with me, if I were so inclined.'

'Well,' Charles Rose laughed.

'Everyone is watching us,' Simone said with delight.

'Every move you make,' Charles Rose replied, 'is eminently worth watching.'

This remark was proving truthful, at least so far as concerned Émilien Surville, who held fresh in his memory that gambit, pregnant with ambiguity, that Simone had made just before Princess Cécile granted her leave. What was this artist doing sticking her nose into this business anyway? Well, too bad. Surville had seen all he needed, and once he realized as much he left the embassy. The valet pulled up in his brand-new Anderloni coupe (same model as the resplendent mustard-yellow number he'd owned until its unfortunate theft on Old Port Road just a few weeks earlier). The loss of his old car still smarted, particularly since the mustard-yellow option had been dropped from the still-extensive range of colours available from the Anderloni factory. He sat in his new coupe a few seconds, deep in thought and glancing from time to time at the embassy building, before starting the engine and speeding resolutely toward the edge of town, where a once prosperous commercial district was in the throes of slow decay. Arriving in this hinterland, he stopped on the vacant, cracked asphalt of a recently decommissioned service station near which, Surville knew, a certain phone booth was bravely resisting the march of progress.

Our man entered the booth, where he was thrilled to find a current phone book. He sang the praises of the phone company and started looking for the page that, according to a double-entry system committed to memory, matched the current day of the week. His luck held: the page hadn't been torn out, as was ever more frequently proving to be the case since his bosses devised this system of clandestine communication. Surville found the correct column (for the month) and range (the day), double-checked everything, then dialled the number of a certain Mutt R. As agreed, the phone rang seven times before a click made it clear that he had been connected.

'I have information on Mansaré.'

'Go on,' said the voice at the other end.

'Inform our people that he's no longer alone in the field. He has,' said Surville, with that blush of pride one feels upon unearthing a savoury morsel of intelligence, 'an accomplice.'

True to her promise, Simone hooked Sarah-Jeanne Loubier up with Alban Wouters, and the morning agreed upon by the gallery owner to look over her portfolio arrived.

A week before, Sarah-Jeanne Loubier had gone to Simone's house. Since their unplanned meeting in the Porte du Midi, she had seriously pruned her portfolio and also added a new series of pastels, in a palette of judiciously dark hues that threw into relief the rare bold lines of vibrant colour, always near the edges of the sheet, as if for Sarah-Jeanne Loubier a drawing's centre could only ever hold an absence. Simone had looked them over and suggested an even more pared-down selection. Then they had dinner and white wine.

Alban Wouters reluctantly flipped through the drawings, secretly disappointed. He'd hoped this young apprentice so lauded by Simone might share the older artist's choice of subject. Sure, there were a few nudes in the lot, but there was an ineffable, almost lunar quality about them, as if fated to wane. Of course, Alban Wouters didn't expect all figurative artists to produce erotica. But erotica sold, it had to be said, just as it had to be said that, even with all the talent in the world, this young Sarah-Jeanne Loubier had not yet made a name for herself.

Sarah-Jeanne was trying to contain her nerves at the obdurate silence of the man occupied at that very moment with casting his cranky eye over the body of work on which she had pinned all her hopes. 'Above all,' Simone had stressed, 'always stay calm. Don't ever panic. Alban may seem a little gruff, until you get to know him. He likes to put on a gruff face. It's just business. His tough-guy act is just a front. Don't try to sell him; give him time. Alban loves to believe he's discovered something for himself.'

So Sarah-Jeanne kept quiet, and perhaps it was that unflinching silence, somehow mirroring the gallery owner's own, that favourably impressed Alban Wouters. He owed Simone one, this too had to be said. And it truly was a wonderful portfolio.

'Okay,' he began. 'I should tell you upfront, I almost never take on young artists. We could stop there: I could tell you that you aren't the first, that you still need to hone your craft, form a collective of like-minded artists maybe, I don't know, join an artist-run centre, and I'll keep a keen eye on your progress, your budding career, and who knows, maybe one day … But you've put an idea in my head.' (Here he stood up, to squeeze the full dramatic potential from the coming speech.) 'Emerging artists, emerging artists: one can't simply sit around waiting for them to emerge all on their own. They need our support. Opportunities. Opportunities in the institutions where we hold sway … Like this gallery.'

Here Alban Wouters made a sweeping gesture that spanned the main gallery, currently occupied by a retrospective of an abstract painter, recently deceased, whose death had coincided with a renewed interest in his oeuvre.

'This exhibition finishes next week. Then the gallery will close for a few days, and I'll improve the signage inside. No one can ever seem to find the backroom.

'There's a backroom?' asked a surprised Sarah-Jeanne Loubier.

'Exactly. It's been like that ever since I set it up. But don't worry about that, I'm not here to. Listen. It's nothing fancy, I'm planning a little group show in the fall. Would you like to be part of it?'

'Seriously?' asked Sarah-Jeanne, lighting up.

'Nothing but drawings,' Alban Wouters went on. 'More and more of my artists seem to have drawerfuls of them. But I can't really see an entire exhibition. Or else you'd need to fill it out, put out a monograph, drum up some press … It's only with Simone that. But then Simone's different. Long story short, drawing is back. There's no denying it. It's all you see in the art mags these days. Look, I can't say how it'll go over with my clients. They have their habits, after all. But if we never take a chance.'

'That's …' said the resplendent Sarah-Jeanne.

'It's not much,' grunted the gallery owner, still keeping up appearances. 'I'll take two pieces, max. And it'll be in the backroom. You'd better hope the agency I've hired for the signage is as talented as they claim.'

Faya had no keys, no cash, and no ID. She walked along in scuffed sandals, exhausted and aimless. The city was a blur, the atmosphere a ball of cotton, the very existence of sidewalks and the people who were walking on them and the shop windows they looked into had become a matter of conjecture.

She came to a bridge and crossed over to the side with a view of the marina in the foreground, the silos and shipyard beyond. On the other side of the bridge, a canal ran into the city and then out again, over a series of locks, to join up with the southern valleys and, surely, some inland sea. A barge floated by. Faya thought about jumping onto it. And then it was gone. Should she jump anyway? The question crossed her mind.

Similar thoughts continued to beset Faya as she walked over the level crossing. But no train deigned to appear in the ten full minutes she spent above the track, lazily perusing the plant life wilding the sides of a factory whose red brick was interspersed with broken windows behind metal grilles, until a stranger approached and was bold enough to address her with a few words that, by the time they reached Faya, were degraded to the point of unintelligibility, shapeless collections of hisses and fricatives over a background somewhere between feedback and interference, and in answer to which she cried out, swore, ran away, then yelled and swore some more.

Not far-off, in a fifth-floor apartment of a narrow building perched on the edge of an alleyway paved with shadows, The Bear was working on his needlepoint. He had pushed his desk under the little window through which he liked to observe the activity at the port. Every wall was burdened with shelves overflowing with yellow-paged volumes. A solitary sofa with threadbare upholstery sat waiting to be read on. A record player in the corner was cranking out an interpretation of a standard for alto sax, trumpet, and drums (*All Night No Luck*, Sonatine Records S-3389). The Bear scrutinized his handiwork. At that very moment he heard the hoarse crackling of the intercom. He wasn't expecting anyone, but left the needle stuck in the canvas, took the few steps required to reach the doorway, then pressed the button marked *DOOR* without bothering to see who it was: a wrong address, probably; a neighbour who'd forgotten the code, perhaps. The album ended and The Bear turned the radio on. A man was deep in impassioned parlay in Creole with another. Finally The Bear heard a knock on the door.

It was surprising to see Faya appear at his door and then unceremoniously cross his apartment and lock herself in the bathroom; more surprising still to see her come out, ten minutes later, dressed only in her panties.

'I stink. I'm sure I stink. Can you tell me if I stink?'

The Bear, who as it happened had a virtuosic sense of smell, took a few puffs of Faya's neck. Nothing special. It just smelled like human.

'So it's my clothes then,' Faya deduced.

The Bear offered to take them down to the laundry room. 'Make yourself at home,' he suggested, before heading down the stairs with a little plastic bag of dirty clothes, one step after another all the way to the basement, where a dozen machines awaited the clink of coins to trundle into motion. Along the way he wondered what place the word *home* might conjure up in Faya's mind. He went back up the stairs (they'd been promising to fix the elevator for six months). In his absence, Faya had borrowed a T-shirt way too big for her and was staring in wonder at a cumbia LP (*Medianoche en el trópico*, Carga Roja Records 772). But Faya wasn't dancing. She did not tap a foot, or even nod her head; she just sat on the floor, leaning on her right arm, knees bent halfway, absent. The Bear asked if she had had lunch and moved toward the gas stove, where he cooked an omelette. When he came back he found her reading Volume 2 of *The Universal History of Cryptography and Passwords (Illustrated)*. He put her plate down next to her; she scarfed down the entire meal, though only after scrupulously removing every trace of mushroom. (The Bear discreetly fed on them when he carried the dish to the kitchen sink.)

'Want anything else?' he asked.

She made a gesture in which it would be hard to read even a hint of enthusiasm. The Bear tried a few more times to stoke the flames of conversation, without success, and then retreated to his desk. He was troubled by Faya's presence, and on his first attempt he pierced the fabric with his needle a few millimetres wide of the mark. Then, in the attempt to pull it out, he hurt himself. 'Oww!' he exclaimed. Faya didn't react. And yet, and yet, he ruminated.

He did manage to embroider a few cross-stiches. Slowly his X was taking shape. One great X made of countless little x's, he thought, not hearing Faya tiptoe over, somehow sidestepping the floorboard in the middle of the room that always creaked.

'What are you doing?' she asked, suddenly interested. 'Oh, needle-point! Looks boring.'

The Bear had no idea how to dispel this assertion, whose accuracy was hard to dispute. Boredom was an agreeable condition to him. Faya leaned in closer, until she was straddling his left thigh.

'You're hot. I never noticed how hot you are. And I'm ugly. Tell me I'm not ugly.'

'What a question!' exclaimed the bewildered Bear. 'Of course you're not ugly.'

'I want to sleep with you,' she said.

It was entirely unexpected.

(Although ...)

(In the end, it was as though Faya had rediscovered her teasing ways, that characteristic stubborn streak she seemed to have lost in recent months, since the night of the Poupée Sincère concert when Simone left her, to be exact. For a moment The Bear clung to this idea of remission, though he soon had to give it up. There were no two ways about it, something was wrong. Faya wasn't herself anymore.)

(And yet, and yet …)

They kissed. There was no resisting. He picked her up and gently laid her down on the bed. He caressed her. She felt good, soothed down to the deepest core of her being, where the cracks were growing harder and harder to conceal from view. Time passed; Faya drifted off. She started snoring gently. The Bear observed her a few minutes longer, full of emotion but actually more relieved than frustrated. Then he left her alone in his bedroom and shut the door.

Night fell. The Bear completed his alphabetic composition.

He put away his sewing materials and turned on the radio, in time for his favourite show, *The Heyday of the Space Race*. He almost forgot his guest's presence. But a languorous murmur reached him from the bedroom, followed by a panicked interjection.

'What time is it?' asked Faya, bolting out of bed. 'Where are my clothes?' She seemed to be a new woman, suddenly herself again, galvanized by an undercurrent of apprehension. Or was it remorse?

'I've got your clothes. They're dry,' explained The Bear, pointing to an immaculately folded pile on the coffee table.

She picked it up and fled to her room again, then re-emerged, clothed and aggrieved.

'Do you know this radio show?' asked The Bear.

'I've gotta go. Célestine will kill me if she finds out where I spent the afternoon.'

'Uh, okay,' said the baffled Bear.

'It's normal, you know. To be jealous, when you're in love. When you care about someone, I mean. And I know she cares about me. She told me so! She told me I'd better not let her down. And she's right. When you love someone, you have to be committed. I've never been with someone like her. The way she makes me. You wouldn't understand. Anyway, it's not my fault if she has friends who.'

'Friends who?'

'Who nothing. Anyway, they're not really her friends. People she knows. Anyway, you never saw me. I never told you anything. Nothing at all, okay. Be well.'

She slammed the door on her way out. The Bear didn't move for a minute. The soft voice of the radio announcer was describing the journey of a space probe currently orbiting the Polenta IV asteroid … but no, The Bear, lost in his thoughts, misheard; no one had named an asteroid, let alone four, after a vulgar slab of corn-flour paste. Goaded by a sudden fear, The Bear left the room and hurtled down his building's stairwell. Outside, he looked left and right – no one. He then chose a direction at random and began searching the neighbourhood, full speed ahead. He saw no sign of her.

He felt bad for taking so long to react. He came back crushed. What had she meant by that 'Be well'? It could mean a lot of things, not all necessarily final. Faya wasn't one to choose her words with care. But there had been more. 'I never told you anything': would he have to stifle this impromptu surge of desire she had kindled in him (and that he still preferred to half-believe in)? Or was it rather a question of Célestine's mysterious entourage, these friends who weren't really friends at all. What hornets' nest had he stuck his paw into?

The Bear opened a door, pulled out a small notebook toothed with alphabetic tabs, found a phone booth, and dialled Pierre-Luc's number. Maybe he'd know what to do. But no one picked up. 'I wanted to talk to you about something,' said The Bear after the beep. 'It's Faya. It might be nothing. I'll try to catch you later.' The Bear hung up. He was already wondering if the call was a mistake. Mainly, and confusedly, he wondered if the sensible course might not be to say nothing at all.

No matter how insistently they made their case, it was no use: Fabrice Mansaré refused to say a word about the Sorgue File, and instead seemed determined to relate, in excruciating detail, an obscure episode from his youth: three weeks spent with his sister Alice in the family anti-nuclear bunker.

The truth serum gave him glassy eyes and a bewildered gaze, tempered by a slight droop in his eyebrows. He spoke quietly, in a high-pitched voice. Soon he'd have no memory of this little session.

That afternoon, he said, the phone had rung at General Mansaré's home, a house with white arcades and a clay tile roof peacefully set far from any neighbour on a hillock of wheat-coloured grass on a windy road in an affluent (and closely guarded) suburb of Port Merveille. Alice picked up the phone. She was reading contentedly on a sofa, a pedestal fan at her feet churning the rare wisps of warm air into an only slightly cooler breeze.

Young Fabrice was floating in the pool. He'd done a few lengths, then stopped straining. He stared skyward where here and there a little lamb leapt; his gaze tracked the white trail of a supersonic jet. From time to time an ibis emitted three raspy syllables, counterpoint to the call of the fantail warbler. When he went back up, he saw his sister with a serious expression on her face. Their father had issued urgent instructions. It was war, she said. The big war.

The entrance to the shelter, they knew, was at the edge of the yard. Until today they'd never once been allowed inside; the shelter's very existence had long been a source of fear and desire. Fabrice looked one last time at the baobab, still conversing with the harmattan; he wondered what would remain after the bomb.

With both hands, Alice turned the airlock open, let her brother go in first, then slipped in and carefully closed the door behind them. They located the light switch and explored the premises. Everything they could ever need was there: books, canned food, chocolate, bedding, alcohol, drinking water, olive-oil soap, a first-aid kit; one cupboard even held a stock of board games. It took them a while to notice that the shelter had no television, radio, or any other means of following the progress of the conflict.

Fabrice was worried about Maguette, the cleaning lady, who must have gotten to the house around the time their father called.

He imagined her vapourized by the conflagration, transformed from one second to the next into a white skeleton. He knew what fate awaited those who tarried on the surface. But it was too late to go out. General Mansaré's orders were not open to discussion.

On the other side of the laboratory's one-way mirror, people were wondering where exactly the subject was taking them with this meandering anecdote, which had decidedly nothing to do with the matter of the interrogation. Patience was running thin.

But a tall blond woman, who until then had kept to the background, cut off the annoyed technicians. She was the one known as Problem 30 in some circles; in others, people called her Célestine.

'You asked him about his last trip to Port Merveille,' she explained, 'and his mind slipped back to another unconnected memory set in the same city. You can't underestimate him. Clearly well-trained.'

'He's wasting our time,' complained one of the technicians.

'Let him talk. This shelter story is interesting. You never know, it may prove useful.'

Still in the serum's grip, Fabrice Mansaré continued his account of his first week in isolation. At the beginning it all seemed like a game, a morbid one perhaps, but a game nonetheless. They were waiting for their father or his envoy to make an appearance; it was only a matter of time. Until then, they were as castaways on a desert island equipped with everything they might need. But the smallness of their quarters soon took on an ominous cast. The world's contraction was a source of dread. What would they find when they emerged? They pictured a ravaged landscape teeming with disease, its population rendered infertile by radioactive fallout. After more than a week with no news, they were convinced they would never again see the earth as they'd known it.

In the bowels of this reinforced concrete bunker, every sensation of their nerves and organs was doubled; every sound came to them with an alarming intensity; their skin now transmitted the most subtle of impulses that before would have been attainable only through sustained concentration. A whole new form of excitement bedevilled them. It was exhausting to be ever in the presence of one you knew so intimately, immersed in their vision and their voice, colour and weight, their total physical being. Irresistibly, in this place outside the world, the exhaustion bred of physical proximity could only be transmuted into a desire that would grow increasingly overt with the passage of time.

It began as a game. But they soon discarded all reservations about being seen by the other, touched by the other. Finding themselves in this New Eden, pure and irreproachable, in the unrepressed fullness of adolescence, they decided, with all the seriousness this discovery entailed, that they were in love – a fortunate state, as they would soon be responsible for repopulating a decimated planet.

Behind the one-way mirror, the technicians wiped their foreheads and avoided each other's eyes. Only Problem 30 seemed immune to the awkwardness of listening to this terrible, sticky secret.

'Fertile ground for the psychologists,' she said.

'The Sorgue File must be dear to him indeed,' one of the technicians offered, in a muffled voice, 'if he'd sooner give us this … shameful secret.'

'Maybe he's not as ashamed as you think,' suggested Problem 30. 'He sounds almost wistful.'

Of course, the war hadn't happened. It had never even been declared.

The bomb remained safely on its launching ramp – no one had even considered deploying it.

One day the airlock opened. At first they were scared; they'd forgotten all about the outside world. Someone came down. The woman had slightly tanned peach-coloured skin and short blond hair, and was dressed in a blazer. Fabrice recognized Mademoiselle Jacquet, their father's secretary.

'What are you doing?' she exploded.

And the eyes of them both were opened, and they knew that they were naked. They offered no explanation. They talked about General Mansaré's imperious phone call. The bunker smelled of garbage and dirty skin.

'Put some clothes on,' she ordered. 'Your father is insane. I only today fully realized what he made you do.'

They followed her out of the shelter on stiff legs. The sun and the heat almost knocked them over. Finally they reached the villa and collapsed, each on a sofa. The pedestal fan was still churning the air, just as it had throughout their absence.

'He really put you to the test,' said Mademoiselle Jacquet. 'He was testing you. Especially you, Fabrice. He has plans for you. Do you see?'

She had come nearer and was holding him firmly by both hands. But he was entranced by the secretary's unyielding gaze, a gaze full of goodness that never let the beholder's eye off the hook. A peaceful gaze, devoid of malice, but magnetic, and suggestive of some other form of desire – one that was subtler, more sublime perhaps. Fabrice realized she was unquestionably his father's mistress.

On her sofa, Alice was sobbing like a child waking up from a bad dream, or an exceedingly good one. Mademoiselle Jacquet took her in her arms. 'It's over, little one. This cruel test is over. Forget everything that happened.'

As Charles Rose walked to his rendezvous, he had no memory whatsoever of how he'd spent the morning. Admittedly, the nature of his work had entailed developing a mental self-defence technique that permitted him, when necessary, to reassign certain disagreeable or dangerous sensory perceptions to a sort of limbo in his memory (from whence they threatened to leach upward again one day, no doubt, but then one cannot have it all).

This time was different. He was convinced this amnesia was not of his own contrivance. By deduction he imagined what had happened, and decided to trust a mind as expertly trained for psychic combat as his was. Yet a hazy sense of shame still held him in its clutch. It was like coming home to find your apartment ransacked. The main thing was that he had been released. Undoubtedly his adversaries considered him more useful alive than dead. And let's dispel the myth that people get killed off all the time in our line of work. The world is nasty and brutish enough; there's no need to exaggerate.

For the time being, Charles Rose made his way along the boulevard, one man among many, but the only one on his way to meet a fiancée patiently waiting at the bistro. He hadn't seen Simone in three days and the hiatus was painful. Those two were nothing if not in love. And their wedding was fast approaching.

Recent days had left Simone with little time to pine. First she'd visited the Tournoeil Press, where the first copies of *Ballerina Porteña* were rolling off the presses. She admired the depth of the impress of the characters and the two-tone emerald printing job, and she distractedly caressed a few signatures. Then it was off to the bindery.

But we aren't here to talk about books. After leaving the printer's, Simone went to Neuforth Street, where she located the *hôtel particulier* that was Princess Cécile's current home.

The princess had insisted on seeing Simone that very afternoon. She greeted her new friend with deep affection, taking advantage of her happy presence to dismiss, in a flurry of polite pretext, the film-maker who had come to discuss funding for his project. She simply couldn't abide romantic comedies, the princess admitted to her guest once the auteur had beaten his retreat. They had tea in a miniature arboretum enclosed by three high white stone walls. Under a Nootka cypress they chatted about politics and gender studies, finding a few affinities. (Simone found theprincess's views lacking a certain engagement with the real world, but felt her heart was in the right place.)

After a brief discussion, Princess Cécile got up to deliver instructions for the benefit of her servants. Then the two women were off. A taxi stood waiting. It was time to go shopping.

Simone knew the city well but rarely frequented its *maisons de couture*. She suggested a visit to an eminent jeweller whose gold-leaf doors had had two centuries to build up their patina. But the princess was too familiar with the establishment, had her heart set on something fresher. Simone directed the taxi to a neighbourhood she knew to be full of artisans less staid in outlook and more female in their persons. They were dropped off on a street parallel to the boulevards of the old city, in front of an antique shop specializing in fine collectibles from the past sixty years, or deft copies thereof. Next door was a narrow boutique, the House of Soizic. The Princess was thrilled:

'My god, that dress!'

The window indeed displayed a pleated black dress in a daring cut. They went in. Soizic herself attended to their needs; they toured the workshop behind the store, where the princess couldn't help noticing a few just-finished items not yet offered up for sale and asking whether she might enjoy their exclusive use. The friends left with handfuls of bags.

But their shopping was far from over. From time to time, parcels and bags were dispatched back to Neuforth Street. Swept up in the enthusiasm, Simone made some purchases of her own, but not even in her wildest dreams would she have imagined the princess capable of maintaining this frantic tempo of expenditure.

The financial considerations fluttering through Simone's mind were quelled at the pair's third boutique when the princess, not insensitive to the disparate means of individuals of different stations, insisted on paying for Simone's current and subsequent purchases.

'Not a word!' she insisted. 'It's not as if it's my fortune.'

Prince Ludwig's affluence was not limited to family wealth; he also did brisk trade in diamonds. The princess pronounced the word as if there were something filthy about it.

'And yet you know how fond I am of diamonds.'

On that note they entered a jeweller's. And then another, and another. For thprincess, however, this luxury was quick to pall. She now had a hankering for something more … something less … Simone suggested the surprising vintage clothiers of Old Market Square, which she knew well and were sure to scratch the princess's itch for a slightly seedier experience. But it was then time for the princess's yoga class, followed by a benefit for sick children, with canapés, that she simply couldn't get out of.

'Let's pick up where we left off tomorrow,' was Princess Cécile's edict as she scratched her head before an implacable crocodile-skin agenda. 'I have an hour or two between my hairdresser and my cousin Albert, who's expecting me at one. Too bad for the Hungarian sculptor I commissioned for my husband's bust. So many responsibilities! How I envy you your simple life. I'll have you brought here tomorrow at eleven. We'll meet at the Old Market Square, as you suggest. We'll even have time for a quick lunch.'

A driver brought Simone home along with a dozen bags emblazoned with the most exclusive names, which she waited till evening to carry to her room, there to submit herself to a new session of trying on the embarrassment of iniquitously acquired dresses, suits, blazers, and blouses, flip-flopping between intoxication and nausea at this abundance. Outside the stores, none of it was quite her style. She'd surely end up giving much of it away. And where, pray tell, was one to put it all? Her closets were full. She lay down on the bed still covered with new purchases and masturbated heartily, thinking of Charles Rose, and of others as well, and not unmoved by the sight of herself in the mirrored door of the open wardrobe.

She slept fitfully.

The next day was rainy. The Old Market, mercifully, was of the covered sort, with tarpaulins stretched to protect its stalls from precipitation. Junk men and antique sellers and bookstallers haughtily sized up passing customers with a seasoned eye. Around the public square, purveyors of telecommunications devices and other technological gimcracks plied their trade alongside haberdashers, cordwainers, and rarity-hawkers. A sparse crowd weaved around rain puddles. The princess professed her delight over a piece of English chintz in pink-and-violet floral motifs on an aquamarine background. She fell in love with a cream muslin dress with a leaf print of the same emerald as her eyes, going for a pittance. She was bowled over by grey leather high-heeled boots with open-work embroidery. For a full hour she filled the frippers with perplexity and delight. Simone suggested they broaden their culinary horizons and delve even deeper into the realm of the commonfolk, so they lunched on *Flammeküchen* in a brasserie with a view on the Old Market Square, gladdened by sudden fingers of light piercing the clouds, making the raindrops glisten on the tarps. Princess Cécile took an ecstatic inventory of her purchases. Simone, in silence, felt the limitations of their friendship. A song played on the radio.

> Facing north, I play dead,
> But the sea knows my true heart.
> Facing north, I lose my head,
> Drown in you, my body my art.

The princess approved. She'd heard this ditty earlier on the car stereo and found it very much to her taste. She had even uncharacteristically gone so far as to instruct the chauffeur to tune the radio to a popular music station, she boasted to Simone. How joyful it was to commune with the culture of the commonfolk! Simone yearned to change the subject, but it proved unnecessary: the princess suddenly addressed her in the hushed confidential tones of one preparing to confess something most out of keeping with her high place in life.

'My dear friend,' she said with a blush in her cheek. 'You simply must give me the name of the person who did your tattoo.'

The tattoo. Tucked safely between Simone's shoulder blades, it generally stayed out of sight and mind, save for the machinations of mirrors or contrivances of photography (she had a few recent shots in which the design was visible). But of course Simone was aware that this ornament, or what little of it was exposed by her neckline, was duly noted by the men and women she came in contact with, not to mention potential lovers. The tattoo was a recent work, by a friend of a friend. First Esma Lorca had shown her a sketch: three female demons with caustic expressions marked out by big black praline-shaped eyes, entwined in an arborescence both literal and figurative, as they were surrounded by a proliferation of budding branches as well as, per the dictates of the genre, a few roses – all highly stylized. The nervous, spindly motifs; the overgrown abstraction of the scene; the stunning modernity of the style: all pleased Simone, as did the idea that she might serve as an artist's canvas, at the cost of some small physical discomfort.

Esma Lorca had left her with a few business cards; she passed one to the princess. 'Tell her I sent you,' said Simone, and as she did she fathomed the ridiculousness of the notion that one of such high birth as this would ever stoop to tattooing her flesh.

'Thank you kindly,' the princess said, delicately stowing the card in a cardholder. 'Oh! Good god, it's that time when I turn into a pumpkin. That damn Albert will scold me. No matter, he can wait. Can we drop you off somewhere?'

'I've got errands in the neighbourhood,' Simone lied.

'You've been so kind!' the princess gushed again. 'To spend all this time with me when you have so many people to see. I'm much obliged. Believe me, I do understand what a burden I am to you.'

They exchanged tender kisses on the cheek.

The sky had cleared but promised nothing further. The song Simone had heard at the bistro remained stubbornly stuck in her head. It was, it's true, a catchy number, even with that tinge of sorrow in the chorus. Simone didn't yet know – would she ever? – that it was the Poupée Sincère's first single, just released, called 'Facing North,' a straight-up hit of the kind they just don't make anymore, the kind any program director or DJ worth their salt would recognize immediately. Still, the song, or something that wasn't the song but was perhaps connected to it in some way, reminded Simone of Faya. It got under her skin.

Deep in her own thoughts, she failed to notice the bald man in a buttoned jacket following her and occasionally pulling a Minox from his pocket to take a fresh exposure, trying to capture different angles and different expressions. By the time he was finished, his employers would have a lovely little album with a pleasing variety of shots. The bald man, who believed any job worth doing was worth doing right, applied himself vigorously to the task at hand. In his diligence he failed to notice that he himself was being followed, at least until he felt a stab of pain in his neck, accompanied by the loss of control over his legs. From a hiding place behind a newsstand, a lanky individual in an overcoat put down his raincoat loaded with curare darts and pounced upon the little bald man, deftly stealing his camera before disappearing into the open mouth of the metro. Once he reached the platform, the lanky individual took a deep breath, patted the larcenous lump at the bottom of his pocket, and felt a wave of contentment. As the train took its sweet time to appear, he studied the map of the city on the wall, which restored his composure. He got off after three stations, then took a circumlocutory series of buses and taxis, and even purchased a ticket for a Bateau-Mouche.

Proud of his work, he reappeared in a café and went down to the basement, where the phone lived. 'All good,' he said into the handset before leaving the booth and giving his pocket another quick pat, just to be on the safe side, feeling for the camera that had never once left his pocket. A chubby-cheeked man whose raincoat was stretched a little tightly over his girth bumped into him on the way out of the bathroom. The lanky man felt something cold on his back. The two men walked discreetly out of the café and strolled toward the Botanical Garden like two close and slightly agitated friends. Under the canopy of a broad-limbed Senegal mahogany that attracted few people on this cold, wet weekday, the chubby-cheeked man whose raincoat stretched a little tightly over his girth knocked the lanky man unconscious with the butt of his revolver, then took off with the coveted camera. A car was waiting not far from the Museum of Natural Science, which was closed for renovations. The chubby-cheeked man walked briskly toward the car, climbed in, and signalled to the driver, who took off without a word. 'I'm getting too old for this,' he sighed, not without pride at being in a position to appear at the embassy with the compromising pickings. 'Hold on,' he said, 'this isn't the way to the embassy.' 'No it isn't,' confirmed the driver, a stocky man in glasses and a button-up jacket.

Charles Rose was already seated when Simone walked into the bistro where they'd agreed to meet. She apologized, looked somehow absent. He too seemed preoccupied with something unrelated to their love. They ordered, then looked each other over, in search of a door into conversation. It was as if part of the magic were gone, they noticed simultaneously as silence descended. If crack there was, it must be swiftly filled. Say something right away, something surprising or a little dangerous, usher in some perilous new adventure. Simone believed that love, like art, consisted above all in tension. She stood up, excused herself to go freshen up. When she got back, she took the seat beside her fiancé rather than the one across from him. Drinks had appeared. 'We completely forgot to kiss,' she said. 'An egregious omission,' he agreed. They remedied the situation. It took three minutes. 'You do know,' mentioned Charles Rose, 'that making love in public bathrooms is frowned upon.' 'A crying shame,' murmured Simone. 'And what would you say,' Charles Rose said with a smile, 'to a few days of vacation?'

In his office in the Port Merveille presidential palace, a furious General Mansaré sat listening to the local news. He didn't like what he was hearing. But there was no easy way to turn it off, trussed as he was to his chair.

Two masked rebels had their guns trained negligently on the general, while a third perused a bar that would have been considered well-stocked at the best of times, let alone in this period of nationwide shortages.

The radio reported that Parliament had fallen to the rebels, whose advance into the capital was no longer a matter of conjecture. A sizable faction of the army – trained, the general happened to know, by that damned Sorgue – had already symbolically laid down their weapons. The people would likely be quickly won over to the cause, then disillusioned shortly thereafter (but ancillary considerations of the universal history of political revolutions were not among General Mansaré's immediate concerns).

The old general had anticipated the possibility of this revolt, made preparations, sent emissaries hither and yon. His manoeuvrings had secured the grudging military support of a handful of foreign powers. It wasn't much. And in exchange he'd had to hold his puppet President Chénier to a few vague human rights concessions and promises of reform, which made equally indistinct waves in the international press. Behind closed doors there had been talk of his nation's main extractive resource, diamonds. The groundwork for a counterstrike had been laid – with one possible exception that wracked the general with worry. His son, Fabrice, should have been in touch long ago. Where was that good-for-nothing boy? What was the status of his mission? The general grimaced. He didn't speak; his kidnappers were equally laconic, save the third man who kept right on with his inventory of the well-stocked bar.

The radio host, already as nervous as a player on the day of a big game, announced that a story of the utmost importance would be dropping any moment; he then confusedly stuttered a few words he'd been passed on a crumpled piece of paper, and it dawned on him that he was being ordered to step away from the microphone by the rebels, who had now taken over every floor of the national broadcaster's headquarters and were making ready to pre-empt the regularly scheduled news. This insubordination at the state organ was immediately incarnated in the soulful gravelly voice of Doualé Bocandé, famous griot who was in theory blacklisted from Port Merveille's airwaves , and whose protest song 'Coupez Coupez' had swept the nation as the anthem of the revolution.

Almost at that exact moment, the city's police headquarters exploded in a horrific fracas. Grey smoke was visible as far away as the foothills of Port Merveille, where General Mansaré's villa still stood, white paint peeling on the arcades under the worn clay tiles of the roof. Maguette, the old maid, was running around the servants' wing, beseeching all to run for their lives.

And soon enough, whipped into a frenzy by battle-ready insurgents, an enraged and desperate crowd mobbed the forbidden heights of this obscenely wealthy neighbourhood, armed with sticks, torches, and probably the odd rifle. Yellow grass dried by the pounding sun burned in their wake. The flames billowed up along with the fierce rumble of voices as the hoarse whisper of roaring flames engulfed the villa where Fabrice Mansaré had grown up and first fallen in love.

The disciplinary committee hadn't gone badly, all things considered. If Pierre-Luc had lost his teaching job, it was in no way the fault of the dean, or his department head, or even the head of HR, to say nothing of the psychologist. Everyone had been perfect pictures of empathy.

The committee first questioned Pierre-Luc, with the greatest tact, on his reasons for missing work. For weeks now, students had complained of coming to class only to find no teacher for their drawing course. No one expected such behaviour from Pierre-Luc, whose professionalism had never been anything short of exemplary. It was true, they knew, that Pierre-Luc was not averse to certain methods that might in fairness be called experimental, and the committee was in full agreement that it could be salutary at times to let the youth figure things out for themselves; still, a little notice would have gone a long way. But no, that wasn't it at all. Pierre-Luc had not been driven by a thirst for pedagogical innovation. 'What then?' asked the psychologist, in a tone of benevolence so true and perfect it seemed almost phony, which it wasn't.

'I took a new job,' Pierre-Luc said. 'I'm working nights.'

Here we must backtrack a few weeks. It started with Pierre-Luc's efforts to make his class meaningful, the very efforts that made him such a beloved educator. At the beginning was the project, one carried out afresh each year, of a student exhibition for the members of the drawing class.

'The show is usually held in the main hallway, as you know. But this year there were grumblings. The students wanted something a little less ... invisible, I guess? To get off the school grounds, at the very least. It sounded like a great idea to me.'

So far the committee was on board. There was no denying that, pleasing though they were to parents and the school administration, there had always been something ersatz about the drawing students' group shows. And it went without saying that an event out in the world would be great visibility for the art school.

So there you had it. A student (Pierre-Luc did not name Sarah-Jeanne Loubier) had suggested the Carouge, a dive bar she knew. (Here Pierre-Luc also omitted the Poupée Sincère concert and ensuing debauched night with Faya and The Bear, to say nothing of the morning after.) The bar had a wall for the work of local artists. A quick phone call sealed the deal. The space was free in two weeks' time.

So far, in the unanimous view of the Disciplinary Committee, this was all perfectly above board. After all, the intramural excursion had been duly approved by the relevant authorities.

'Let me finish,' Pierre-Luc answered nervously.

There remained the music. Vera Vetiver, proprietor of the Carouge, asked Pierre-Luc whether he'd arranged music for the evening. Pierre-Luc passed on this request to the class; one student had a friend who was a DJ. Perfect, one thing fewer to worry about (what with the posters, invitations, food). Yet, the very morning of the opening, Pierre-Luc received a call from the apologetic student, who was sorry but what could you do, the DJ friend had a wedding that same evening, and no gift of ubiquity – I mean, really, what could you do? Back to square one, in short. 'I'll take care of it,' Pierre-Luc reassured the student.

Because it so happened that Pierre-Luc had a record collection that could in all fairness be described as serious. It was his secret garden, not something he was given to showing off for all to see. His stylings of choice were soul, funk, and hard bop – plenty of fodder for a fun opening. Pierre-Luc looked to the committee for approval; the committee approved. And was it not apt for the teacher to disappear behind the turntables, leaving the spotlight to fall on the artists and their guests, this being, after all, their show.

All this to say the night was a success. People had a lot of fun, several of them even coming up to congratulate Pierre-Luc on the great tunes. What's more, they danced. For this, too, he had come equipped with all his sharpest numbers: rare surf and boogaloo pressings, timeless jazz classics, voices of sandpaper and satin, explosive base, breakneck rhythms, criminally catchy choruses. As the evening drew to a close and midnight approached, the proprietor herself came over to give Pierre-Luc props and a pint of pale ale, and to inquire whether he might be available to DJ the odd weeknight, paid of course, drinks at staff price. Pierre-Luc took a swig of beer. He was touched by the invitation and didn't think twice. Only the next day did it dawn on him that this new occupation might intrude on his teaching schedule.

'You have to understand,' he justified himself to the Disciplinary Committee, 'I had to give it a shot. At least one night.'

Everything went fine at first. Pierre-Luc had free rein at the Carouge. The week started off quiet, but from Wednesday on, people came to dance, and this new DJ was the answer to their prayers. Every night he came home thoroughly exhausted and content. Mornings were getting tough. The commute to school was torture; his tenosynovitis was growing chronic; he was developing a bothersome case of bruxomania. One morning his brain simply refused to acknowledge the alarm. Pierre-Luc got out of bed mid-afternoon.

Missing work was a revelation of sorts. Riding the tram to the Carouge with his record bag slung over his shoulder, Pierre-Luc realized that his teeth were no longer clenched and his wrist no longer hurt. He was looking forward to another blissful night behind the mixing board. Another morning of 'I'd prefer not to'? Bring it on.

'I think we can all see where this is heading,' Pierre-Luc finished.

'You're exhausted,' came the facile diagnosis of the psychologist, who'd been taking notes as fast as Pierre-Luc could speak. 'On the verge of burnout.'

The other committee members were understanding. No one was here to pass judgment. The school had seen other cases of this kind. They had a comprehensive suite of resources for just such circumstances: paid leave, sabbatical, medical support – all Pierre-Luc had to do was ask. The prospect of a year off was dangling right there in front of him, borne aloft on this surge of well-meaning solicitude.

'I don't know,' Pierre-Luc admitted. 'I was more thinking of resigning.'

'Resigning!' the department head exclaimed.

'Yeah, I'm afraid that, even a year from now …'

Now they had truly seen it all. The school was more than willing to bend over backward to accommodate a staff member, particularly one as well-liked by admin and students alike. But from there to countenancing that one of their own could forsake his secure vocation for this precarious nocturnal hobby, spinning records in some sketchy dive …

Pierre-Luc didn't give an inch. He was trying to let them down as gently as possible. On the other side of the table the faces went from cold to glacial. The Disciplinary Committee didn't appreciate having its time wasted. Finally, the dean came to a decision. Not a decision, exactly, he simply looked at his watch and told the committee he had another appointment. Everyone got up at once. 'I'll be waiting for your letter of resignation, then,' said the head of HR.

Next, Pierre-Luc stopped by his house, got changed (his collection of embroidered-pattern shirts was growing fast), and flipped through some recent acquisitions (his expenditures at second-hand record shops were spiking alarmingly). He was thinking about selling his car. Maybe his house too. He could always get a place in town. *La vie bohème* was calling. He thought of Simone; in a sense, radically changing his life in this way would bring him closer to her. He never saw her anymore.

Sweet Simone …

A slowish Monday night at the Carouge: empty tables, a handful of familiar faces Pierre-Luc was beginning to recognize as regulars.

In between sets he noticed a man sitting in front of an untouched beer, looking like he had nothing to do, not even deigning to remove his buttoned jacket. This man stared back at him, took a sip of beer (or pretended to), and strode over to the DJ booth.

'Do you take requests?' asked the man in the buttoned jacket.

'Not usually,' Pierre-Luc said apologetically.

'Can you play "Facing North"?'

'Look,' said Pierre-Luc, 'I'll see what I can do but.'

'Don't be a jerk,' said the man in the buttoned jacket. 'It's my favourite song.'

Now, transitioning smoothly from a deep soul classic to this ethereal pop confection was no laughing matter. But it was also an opportunity for Pierre-Luc to showcase his chops. First he brought the tempo down a notch and threw in a few electro touches, to blend organic sounds in with some proudly artificial ones, then he took a side trip down the byways of musique concrète, and voila, the stage was set. (There remained, of course, the matter of getting back on track again.)

> The whistle of the narwhal,
> The loneliness of Sunday benches.
> Out there, my regret grows old.
> When will I crack your secret code?

The moment 'Facing North' kicked in, amused faces turned toward Pierre-Luc. A capital joke, they thought. And Pierre-Luc had to admit, it really was a hell of a track. He remembered that Poupée Sincère had been the reason for his first visit to the Carouge, and what a memorable visit it had been. So many coincidences. (It's like we're in a novel.) He thought warmly of Célestine the singer, such an exquisite beauty. Whatever had become of her? And Faya, and The Bear? All these people who come through our lives and then disappear before we have the time to …

Facing north, I flee remorse,
But the sea knows my song by heart.
Facing north, I love you still,
But the sea waits for me at port.

The music lover in the buttoned jacket didn't move from his chair, just nodded his head gently in time to the music. He had opened a steno pad and was noting something down. The song lyrics maybe? Yet the moment he was finished writing he leapt up, left a bill on the table where his untouched beer languished, and walked out. 'How about that,' said Pierre-Luc, disappointed as he began the long swim upstream to his earlier groove, doing his best not to dampen the enthusiasm of the two dancers who had multiplied to four.

He made it. Hours passed; one record followed another; pints were poured and emptied. Around quarter past midnight, Pierre-Luc dropped the needle on a furious eleven-minute Afrobeat number and went outside for some fresh air. That was when he saw Faya.

Faya was walking on the sidewalk across the street, looking at once confused and determined. Pierre-Luc wasn't at first sure it was really her; he soon realized it could be no one else: that hair, that blue raincoat, that plucky strut. He wanted to wave, but she was staring in the other direction. Reluctant to call out her name, he watched as she marched off into the indifferent night. At that moment, a black sedan came out of nowhere and screeched to a halt right next to Faya. Two sinister men emerged. Before Faya had time to react, she was unceremoniously bundled into the car as the engine revved. The whole scene was over in seconds. Pierre-Luc stood watching, paralyzed. Then something deep inside him leapt up, a heroic touch of genius. By coincidence, a cyclist was at that very moment dismounting and preparing to lock up in front of the Carouge. Pierre-Luc commandeered the bike, ignoring the indignant cries of its owner who stood aghast, U-lock still hanging from astounded arm, and took off in unpremeditated pursuit of the vehicle.

'I'll give it back,' he yelled, an assurance that felt more like well-intentioned hope than concrete plan. One legacy of a socialist mayor was that the speed limit on major thoroughfares had been lowered to forty kilometres per hour, which is, as we know, only slightly faster than an experienced cyclist. The route, it must be said, was mostly downhill. And, frankly, Pierre-Luc was on the ride of his life. He soon caught up with the black sedan, temporarily put out of action by a red light, then lost it again, and then found it once more. Pierre-Luc was gaining confidence; he exploded off the line, weaved like an Olympic skier around cars waiting to turn, narrowly missed hitting a truck sliding in between him and his target. Verily was he possessed of supernatural strength and constitution. Within a wheel's length of his prey, he still had no idea what he'd do once he caught up, but that wasn't the issue – what mattered was to not give up. He slid between two lines of waiting cars. He'd made it.

That was the moment chosen by a driver, after successfully parallel parking, to emerge from his car, in contravention of the very basic principles of road safety, without first looking to see what was happening in his left rear-view mirror. Pierre-Luc saw the danger too late and got doored, hard.

The victim wasn't wearing a helmet, The Bear read in the newspaper, dismayed by the insistence on this detail. There's no need to quote here the myriad studies that question the alleged life-saving properties of the bicycle helmet. It all comes down to the type of collision, the source of the impact, and many other factors beside. In any event, the driver came away with only minor mental trauma, the article concluded. At which point The Bear put down his newspaper, and Pierre-Luc came to.

'You were lucky,' The Bear said.

It took the still-dazed Pierre-Luc a while to figure out where he was. The first thing he noticed was that his head hurt, but not in any of the usual headache places; instead, he was plagued by a sort of angry buzzing on the side of the occipital lobe. Next came the discovery that his left arm was immobilized by three centimetres of plaster.

'I came as soon as I heard,' said his friend.

'The bike,' mumbled Pierre-Luc.

'Scrap metal. Someone will take it,' said The Bear. 'On the bright side, you couldn't have landed better. The nurse says your left arm saved you. And the way you took a bounce on the hood of the car, before hitting the pavement. Oh, and you might also have a little discomfort sitting for the next few days.'

Pierre-Luc felt his coccyx's fresh complaint.

'The gods have a soft spot for cyclists,' he concluded.

'Not for cyclists,' The Bear corrected him. 'For idiots.'

Pierre-Luc closed his eyes. He tried to form a mental image of the car that had spirited Faya away. But he couldn't remember the make, wasn't even sure it was black. All the police wanted from him was a licence plate number.

His mission was an unmitigated failure. Today he couldn't even recall the circumstances of the abduction. For all he knew, Faya might have gotten into the car willingly. Could he even say for sure that it was Faya? He didn't tell The Bear what had made him leap onto the bike and start speeding down a busy avenue. A bike that didn't even belong to him, he remembered, tripling his contrition.

'I'm really tired,' he sighed.

The Bear gently placed a paw on Pierre-Luc's shoulder. They said nothing further, and Pierre-Luc dozed off.

When he awoke, The Bear was gone and a nurse was taking his pulse. Daylight filtered through half-drawn white curtains. When it was time for his X-rays, Pierre-Luc enjoyed riding in the wheelchair through hallways harrowed by doctors' footsteps, sometimes catching the murmurings of patients and their families and outbursts of bored children. Being examined, touched, and patted down was an emotional experience. He was given a fast-acting analgesic. The hospital food lived up to its reputation. There was talk of a mild concussion, but he would come out unscathed, albeit with one restriction: no dangerous sports, including urban cycling, without the doctor's permission. At the end of the day he took a few steps on exhausted legs. He looked in the mirror and saw the stitches over his left eyebrow. Night fell.

Pierre-Luc went back to sleep. The next day he woke up very early. His neighbour was still sleeping when a new visitor entered. Shock: it was Célestine, with a bouquet of poppies.

'I don't want to wake you,' she said with concern.

Pierre-Luc forced himself into a sitting position, a manoeuvre that reminded him that his own derrière had not emerged unscathed from its recent contact with the asphalt.

'Oh, flowers!'

'I was really worried about you,' Celestine said. 'How are you feeling?'

'I'll make it,' said Pierre-Luc pitifully. 'If all goes well, they'll let me out this afternoon. Hopefully I've learned my lesson.'

'I'm glad to hear it,' said Célestine seriously. 'And sorry, I am really happy for you. But I'm also worried about Faya.'

'Really?' Pierre-Luc shot out.

'I haven't heard from her in two days,' Célestine continued. 'I'm concerned she might … I mean, you know that she hangs out with some strange people.'

Pierre-Luc remembered The Bear's cryptic voice mail a few weeks ago, which mentioned just these 'strange people.' Crazy how much attention you have to pay to tiny details in this business.

'And you're worried that …' Pierre-Luc said, connecting dots.

'That she may have been kidnapped, yeah,' Célestine confirmed.

Without delay, Pierre-Luc told her the full story of his heroic bike chase. And Célestine in turn filled him in on the sinister brotherhood of General Mansaré's henchmen. A recent putsch, Pierre-Luc learned, had weakened the general's grasp on the military. It had been in the news.

'You know, Faya was born in Port Merveille,' said Célestine. 'We believe she has family connections to certain elements in the – '

'We?'

'I beg your pardon?'

'Why did you say we?'

'It's time I filled you in on a few things,' said Célestine with a sigh.

D rawing is a matter of the eye: you get the prey in your sights, then aim true. And of course it's a well-known fact that killers also work on paper first.

Yet drawing is also a matter of the hand, and that may be where practices diverge. Every artist's signature hand movement transfers onto the page in a singular manner, faithfully transcribing in black on white a highly personal habit of mind.

Take a bucolic scene. A clearing, ringed by wild deciduous trees. At its centre is a duck pond, encircled by a half-hearted bluff of bulrushes where mallards nest with their new broods. Nearby, a field of wheat, perhaps a farm.

Here one artist would construct a scene that may at first glance appear unstudied but is in fact informed by a learned rhetoric of the disposition of planes in space. Ink serves to categorically demarcate things from undivided space. Certain elements, like trees, are flattened and darkened to provide depth of field; others seem animated by a sort of primordial wind, not a crude gust but a veritable breeze whose mildness is tangible. A leaf may fall, in keeping with genus and species. Bushes rise up; wildflowers congregate around them, each unique, with a preference for daisies, lilies, and poppies. The artist's quill will quiver against the paper's texture – one can almost, following along with one's eye, hear it scrape – but the resulting shapes are unequivocal, untamed, and perfectly hermetic. A stronger and fully intentional wobble will reproduce the reflection of bulrushes in a pond crossed by a family of perfectly plump ducks in a neat row, whose anatine obstinacy strikes a comic note. Here and there insects animate the pond banks and undergrowth. In the distance: a farm, freshly plowed fields, a fallen fence post, lying unrighted. Scattered clouds in broken lines suggest the thoughts of the sky.

Only at this point will another artist take out her colours. She rejects out of hand chromatic imitation: instead, a turquoise will serve to edge the trees, violet for the farm, yellow to show up the pond, and green to mark the male denizens of duckland. The lines are thick and rich in texture, vigorously and carefully applied. The scene begins as a shorthand, but soon the hand zeroes in on certain self-selecting details that combine to form a system: the cavity of a tree, in which we can imagine a chickadee's nest; the fresh tracks of a fox, and at the edges of the field a heretofore unnoticed rabbit warren. The odd splash of vivid colour brightens ground already strewn with extravagant leaves. A piece of paper, cut out and glued back on, corrects the pond's edge where an energetic pencil went astray. Pink rushes climb askew around them. Flat patches of colour flesh out the scene: a bluish hue for foliage, a blond for the sovereign sky.

A different artist altogether might ply this same terrain with a whole other patience: each element would be a filiform entry on a comprehensive list, the entire scene translated into a visual language thin in appearance but in fact full to bursting, from the rendering of the farm in the background, which will here be invoked in a plenitude of detail, to the half-opened position of one of the discreet bay windows, to the wood chips scattered randomly around a log in which a hatchet rests. Trees are covered in minutely detailed bark, part of a forest of cross-hatched beech, oak colonized by bryophyte, birches scarcely touched by the Rotring's point except to insinuate the dark asperities of one, the formidable exfoliations of another. Often lines will be tufted with other things: roots blend in with the grasses clandestinely slipped into stubborn rows.

But Simone sketches freely. Part of her may wish to save every detail of this panorama – but what chaos lies that way! On another sheet, the opposite is true: the plants seem formless, she gets lost in a needlessly complex system of shadows. A fresh attempt yields something perhaps more faithful, yet somehow academic. The curve of the rushes around the pond is fraught, unconvincing; no conceivable wind could have had quite that effect. And that farm doesn't look real at all, more like some sort of plastic toy. She starts again. This time it's the ducks that she can't crack.

I should stick to portraits, thinks Simone, sighing.

Simone hiked over mountain paths, sketchbook under her arm, meeting only the occasional small flock of sheep, and then, instead of heading back toward the inn where Charles Rose was surely waiting, decided to take a detour through the old settlement of Collinges-les-Eaux. At one point on the winding road, two customs officers on their rounds raised kepis at Simone. It was true, she thought, that the border was nearby. Funny place for a vacation.

The village square, with paving stones set in concentric circles around a statue of a local hero, was a typical pre-industrial ruin reduced to wax-cast relic before its time, the iris of a town built in the shadow of a thinly wooded mountain. The water of the stream that ran beside the town had been bottled, once upon a time; together with the thermal baths, it provided the district's livelihood.

Simone stopped at a year-round market stall and bought a basket of strawberries. At the newsstand where the papers gathered, she checked the headlines. In international news, the provisional government in Port Merveille had made a statement yesterday that failed to capture Simone's attention. She plucked a strawberry from the basket while perusing the overflowing magazine rack. On the cover of *C'est Moi!*, the model looked a lot like Faya. In *Neue Pop* she saw a name, Poupée Sincère, which 'held the secret code for music fans around the world,' according to the storied rag. Oh happy day, they had *Revue des Arts*. She asked the vendor for a copy, and took the *Neue Pop* while she was at it. Simone paid and slid her purchases into her sketchbook.

Across the square, who should appear but Charles Rose. He didn't see Simone. Nor was Simone's fiancé alone: a nervous man with curly black hair walked beside him, in a black raincoat and eyeglasses that didn't suit him at all. They took a minute to admire the old stones, then crossed the square and disappeared into a café.

Simone wasn't surprised to see her fiancé with a stranger. He'd chosen their holiday destination, after all; it wasn't implausible that he might have business here. She was irked that he hadn't seen her, though. Even if one side of the newsstand partially hid Simone from view.

Well, she thought, walking toward the café, I'll surprise him. She slipped between the chairs on a half-empty patio – high season wasn't upon them yet – and walked in.

The cramped little café held a handful of people, regulars clearly, clustered at the bar, throwing out darts of conversation and the odd cry of indignation. Neither Charles Rose nor his mysterious companion were anywhere to be found. Simone's entry was met with a pregnant, surprised silence. She decided to wait for a table, where she set down her basket of fruit and ordered a café au lait. Lost in private contemplation, Simone ate a few strawberries, then got up and asked where the washroom was. The waiter's arm showed the way: at the back.

The toilet stall had been built in a sort of courtyard hidden from neighbours' eyes by low walls on two sides, the woods on the third, and the mountain beyond. Simone set off into the woods. On the carpet of pine needles she noticed a few cigarette butts and a scrap of paper evidently ripped from the label of a can. On the back was the handwritten name of a ship. It meant nothing to her. What was all this? Like a pawn in a game, Simone was drawn further into the dark woods. She soon came upon a puddle of mud with a footprint, clearly fresh. Following these clues led Simone to a path. She took one last look back at the café door. No one seemed to have noticed her excursion.

Yes, this was a path, no doubt about it: a bed of pebbles and gravel crunched underfoot as the incline grew steeper. All of a sudden, as if aware of the perils of altitude, the trees dispersed. Simone took a moment to catch her breath. The slope grew steeper still, this time through the open. Up in the heights she intuited the presence of a mountain path she might reach with relative ease by pressing forward in a straight line. There she saw what looked like two men walking. From a distance Simone recognized Charles Rose's pelisse and the unknown man's raincoat. For a few minutes now she'd suspected that something not quite kosher was going on. Then she remembered that the mountain crest marked the international border.

After a few more minutes of climbing, she reached a road lined with gentian and buttercups. The two men had pulled farther ahead. She followed them from a distance, annoyed to be so visible in the middle of this sloping meadow. Charles Rose had to have noticed her following them but did not betray it by a single gesture. Simone grew increasingly upset.

This pursuit went on for a good half-hour. The landscape grew rocky. The path wended on. From time to time, a hoary tree grudgingly gave a hint of shade. Simone was thirsty. She wondered if she might stumble upon the mountain spring the innkeeper had gushed about. Then she saw that she'd lost the two men from sight. It was as if they'd gone off the road or possibly hidden themselves behind a ledge. She kept walking. Yes, a pass in the mountain seemed to open up off in the distance. It looked just wide enough for a traveller with reason to bypass the border hut.

Simone turned around. The two border patrolmen reappeared and again waved their kepis at Simone, the gesture a touch less friendly this time than at their first encounter, when she'd been innocently wandering the road to Collinges-les-Eaux. Of course, she was now on the very road it was their duty to patrol.

She improvised.

'Finally. What a relief to see you. I think I'm lost!'

Simone had affected a shrill, unnatural voice. One of the agents was visibly raising his right eyebrow. His colleague remained impassive.

'I was trying to find the spring,' she explained nervously, 'you know, the mineral spring. I must have taken a wrong turn and now, like a fool, I've lost sight of the village!'

'You're very lost indeed,' said the border patrolman with the expressive eyebrows. 'The spring is way on the other side of the mountain. But it's fenced off. You can't really see it.'

Simone breathed. As long as she could pass for a bewildered tourist, she could buy Charles Rose a little time.

'Oh, really?' she exclaimed. 'But why?'

'That's the way it is,' the border patrolman explained.

'Too bad,' said Simone with an exaggerated disappointment. 'And here I was, so keen to do some drawings!'

Without thinking, she gestured toward the sketchbook she no longer carried. It had been left with her basket of strawberries on the table of the café where she'd followed Charles Rose and his companion. For a fraction of a second she was honestly astonished by her own carelessness.

'My sketchbook. Wherever has my sketchbook gone?'

The two border patrolmen mechanically began inspecting the roadside, as if the object in question had only moments earlier dropped from its owner's arms. Simone tried to forget her subterfuge – the sketchbook was, after all, very dear to her – but it was stronger than she was. Panic set in. At that very moment, she heard a familiar voice.

'Darling! There you are! At last!'

It was Charles Rose, alone this time. In a few quick strides he joined the group. From where?

'My sweet!' he crooned, in the tone of a silly man, larded with paternal condescension. 'I told you to wait for me. It's so easy to get lost in these mountain paths!'

'My sketchbook,' was all she could think to say. 'I've lost my sketchbook.'

'You must have left it in the village square,' he said firmly. 'I'm sure someone picked it up.'

'Could we see your papers, please?' asked the border patrolman who had up to that point been the impassive one.

As it happened, the passports of Simone Agnès Bergmann and Louis Marie Charles Rose were perfectly in order.

'Collinges-les-Eaux is that way,' grunted the border patrolman, pointing a finger at a fork in the road a hundred metres off. 'And I'd like to remind you that you're a stone's throw from an international border.'

Simone and Charles Rose took their passports, thanked the men sycophantically, and set off, hand in hand, toward the road.

'You were marvellous,' said Charles Rose. 'We could have heard you five miles away.'

Simone smiled but didn't answer. She still felt a tad put out.

Charles Rose casually undertook to explain the slightly sticky situation of his client, a communist leader with a big mouth in whom the police, in their infinite discernment, were showing a close interest. Getting him over a border the usual way was impossible; a foreign government had asked for his assistance, and bending the rules of border crossing wasn't much to ask, especially since no one would be hurt. Simone asked whether her fiancé took her for an idiot. Charles Rose supplied some additional details.

I left the inn as they arrived. I walked toward the waiting Cholet; Debruyn started the engine. They went into the room where Simone found her sketchbook laid casually on the bed. 'They do nice work,' said Charles Rose.

Simone had nothing against secrets, per se, even less against adventure, but she disliked being made a fool of. Charles Rose acknowledged this. The couple discussed what to do next. Then one of them happened to make a witty remark, and they laughed.

Charles Rose declaimed a smutty quatrain:

> Sweet hot cross buns, how I love to knead your dough!
> My hand draws out sweet sighs, beneath the dress we go,
> To pluck your lyre, waking the ardent glow,
> And kill your sorrows with one lightning blow.

'Is that your handiwork?' said Simone, laughing.

'Well …' answered Charles Rose, blushing.

'My word, a man of many talents.'

'It's a cruel thing to mock your lover!'

'The rhythm's a little thumping. The lexicon, silly in the best way. But the rhymes are fresh as warm bread! Kudos!'

Charles Rose was embarrassed.

'And now that the song is sung,' Simone said, winking, 'what would you say to doing the deed?'

Later that night, they shared their respective pasts. Simone told Charles Rose about her mother's side of the family, the Charpelles, and the strange, unbridgeable chasm that separated her from them. And, without going into too much detail, Charles Rose told Simone about his upbringing in Port Merveille: how at his father's behest he'd finished military academy, how all he had left of his mother was a photograph, how his sister Alice was yanked from his life at a tender age, when their father sent her away to study medicine in the faraway city of Neudorf. This sister married a student from her cohort, and had a girl named Eugénie. All he knew of his niece was the drawing he'd received when she was four and a half, and which he'd never failed to bring along on his many moves around the world. The drawing was getting old. Eugénie was over twenty now. But what did it matter, sighed Charles Rose. Whence this swell of melancholy? Some facet of Charles Rose's past eluded his understanding still.

Simone chose to pass over in silence the story of her marriages. She'd had three husbands and felt no need to subject Charles Rose to the litany. What would their names – Dorian Kessler, Patrice Perronier, René-Laurain de la Patte – mean to him anyway? Simone sighed. Her memories of these men were not all pleasant. And that was when she made a promise, which she also guarded for herself: Charles Rose would be the final entry on this list.

Vacations are as vacations do: they never fail to slip by too fast. So Simone found herself back at home in the large white house with green trim. The red light on the answering machine had dutifully blinked throughout her absence; the first call was missed just moments after Charles Rose came to pick her up. The caller was Pierre-Luc; the message, confused. 'I found Faya,' he said, 'sort of, okay not really, it's more that I know where they're hiding her, I'm looking for her, she's caught up in some crazy scheme, I was on the wrong track but I've figured it out, there you go, gotta run, I think it's my contact again, beeeeeep!' Faya, Simone thought guiltily. The next missed call, from the Bruant Public Library, listed off a number of overdue works of social science. Faya, thought Simone again, though with a rather different feeling. Then there was another message: the gifted tattoo artist Esma Lorca asked Simone to come by ASAP, she had something important to discuss, in person would be best.

The tattoo studio Esma Lorca shared with two other artists was on the ground floor of a small brick building, tucked in among the vintage clothing stores and pubs of a venerable working-class neighbourhood of Bruant. It lay on the tram route; Simone appeared mid-afternoon, and Esma Lorca suggested they get a coffee, she had a good hour before her next appointment. They ordered. Simone reflexively took out her sketchbook, opened it to the first empty page, and started sketching the tattoo artist, who possessed a beguilingly perfect head of thick black hair abruptly severed just above shoulder level. Simone rendered it in broad strokes applied with the side of her pencil, a technique also used to demarcate Esma Lorca's huge black eyes, behind which Simone couldn't help but detect an unasked question, looming.

'You have to tell me where they all came from. All these high-society ladies.'

'High-society ladies?'

'Look,' continued Esma Lorca. 'I'm not complaining, they're good people. Big tippers. All first-timers, though, you have to hold their hands. And of course every last one of them feels the need to swear up and down that they're no strangers to pain.'

'Princess Cécile.'

'She was the first, yeah,' Esma Lorca confirmed. 'When she showed up with her little dog and camera crew, I thought there must be some mistake. Then she dropped your name. Said all kinds of nice things about you. I hear you're getting married, by the way.'

'In less than a week,' Simone admitted. 'I haven't told anyone, you know me.'

'Right, right, no one but Princess Cécile,' Esma Lorca clarified. 'Who doesn't think twice about upping my prices, even whispered in my ear that if I wanted to attract "the right clientele" I should raise them across the board – tenfold!'

'The right clientele …' Simone began to understand.

'So the next day a new lady comes in my shop. Lady Waddington. Unforgettable, that one. And guess what everyone's saying, in these high-society circles? That I'm the one who did the work on the shoulder of Princess Cécile's bosom buddy, and would I be willing to give them the same treatment? Because it's the dernier cri, all of a sudden. Now that gets me thinking a bit. And I tell myself, gee, Simone really does run in some funny circles.'

'A total coincidence,' Simone objected, amazed. 'I had a few of your cards, and –'

'And then,' Esma Lorca interrupted, 'it was the Duchess d'Abrantès. I'm not even telling you what she had done. His Grace the Duke is in for quite a surprise, I'm sure. But then you know how those types never sleep in the same rooms. My god, what a gossip! The duchess was kind of fun, actually. We talked a lot. She gave me some advice. Anyway, all this to say that ever since this started I haven't had a moment's rest. First there's General Silke von und zu Dovemülle, coming in tomorrow. And the following day, let's see, oh yeah, Head of the Privy Council. Did I mention the maharajah's wife?'

'I get it,' said Simone at last. 'You're messing with me.'

'Oh, it'd be a great joke,' the tattoo artist agreed. 'I wish it were. Truth is, I have so many gentlewomen on my hands I can barely slot them all in. What am I supposed to do – start turning away regular clients? And my colleagues are all getting jealous. I'm not complaining, it's all ching-ching ka-ching. I'm going to buy the building, upper floors and all. On the advice of the clever financial advisor the Duchess d'Abrantès sent my way. Nice guy! And free of charge, no less. We'll have to renovate. We'll be turning the upper floor into a quiet pied-à-terre for Madame. The duke has one, why shouldn't she? These high-society folks sure have their own ways of doing things ... On the other hand, the duchess is very interested in my ideas of radical sisterhood. But then you know all this,' she said as she finished her coffee. 'It's all well and good, but I've got a countess showing up any minute, this was fun, let's do it again soon?'

Seated in the best armchair in his library, wearing an absinthe smoking jacket, the contemplative prince flipped thoughtfully through the morning papers. He pulled a cigarette from his case and clicked his butane lighter, which he then stood upright on the pedestal table, though it soon fell over against the glass ashtray. The International section informed him that in Port Merveille the rebel forces, after a few setbacks in areas defended by troops loyal to General Mansaré (now at large), had managed to take the Presidential Palace and form a provisional government. Subcommander Sorgue had been named interim leader, President Chénier forced into exile. The nation's neighbours were reserving judgment, waiting to see what happened; Europe was wringing its hands and calling for basic human rights; a dozen ambassadors had been repatriated. These political melees were of no interest to Prince Ludwig, who had but one concern: the 148 carats (and change) of the Supreme Orchestra, which His Highness had a mind to acquire. That this acquisition would fund the martial aims of one side in this conflict was a matter of indifference, though the prince did sense that his sympathies were more closely aligned with the restoration than the insurrection (time would tell what remained of pure ideology at the end of the day). The prince sucked in a luxurious puff of blond tobacco, then stubbed out the butt like some run-of-the-mill skid.

Monsieur Émilien Surville was announced. This mincing courtier was no friend of the prince's, but he had his uses. He'd been keeping an eye on the comings and goings of Princess Cécile, and believed he had seen things that warranted a word with the sovereign: Her

Ladyship was spending altogether too much time with a certain louche character, to wit, Simone Bergmann, who in an interesting twist was the fiancée of General Mansaré's son, the same son who, as the prince must know, was brokering the sale of the coveted pink diamond; and was the prince also aware that, in his dealings with civil society, the general's son availed himself of a pseudonym that cheekily referenced the colour of that very gem?

Surville's lack of worldliness sent the prince's eyes rolling back in his head. It was a small world, and a smaller demimonde, as Surville must know. And the princess's friendships were notorious. Ludwig remembered the tall, distinguished man whose acquaintance he'd made last winter at the charity reception, whom Princess Cécile had taken such a shine to – a charming fellow, undeniably – and who had turned out to be the twin brother of an anarchist wanted by international police. 'But let's get down to brass tacks, Surville,' he said. 'Give me the facts.' Surville adduced that it wasn't a matter of dubious associations alone: the princess had also been seen spending time in undesirable neighbourhoods, to say nothing of the questionable business underway with a certain Esma Lorca, tattoo artist. 'My wife has always had a soft spot for Bohemians,' the prince explained, his mind uncharacteristically straying from its one true love.

It's not fair, Émilien Surville protested to himself. Here he was going to great lengths in his search to unearth conspiracies, at his very great peril. Recently Surville had begun to feel less self-assured, less confident in his own genius. Was that just an impression? The erosion of his self-confidence could be reliably dated, if his calculations were correct, to the very moment of the unfortunate theft of his mustard-yellow Anderloni, just weeks earlier, a violation he had not gotten over, as if along with the car he had been somehow stripped of the foundations of his strength. A disgruntled Surville reviewed his mental notes, almost wholly concerned with the escapades of Princess Cécile, which were of course a matter of indifference to the prince, a man whose single and abiding passion – diamonds in general – had been channelled into his lust for one diamond in particular. The Supreme Orchestra – rectangular in shape, artisanally and miraculously extracted from the subsoil by unwashed riff-raff – was to be the pièce de résistance of his collection. One day it would adorn the throne of the principality. In matters of aesthetics, we can only say, 'To each his own.'

Concerning the transaction itself, Surville had been provided certain details he was slowly assembling into a complete picture. It had taken time, but a figure had been settled on. The usual terms: hard currency in a suitcase of specific colour and dimensions. Mansaré fils was to wed two days hence. The transaction would take place on the wedding day, early in the morning, in a discreet location to be determined. The diamond would be in a small black case. Surville himself would do the hand-off. The plan was to the prince's liking.

Meanwhile, below the deserted cliffs of Ostden, a small police detachment was curiously watching the tugboat whose crane pulled from uncaring waves the dented hulk of an unlicensed Anderloni, whose flaking paint looked distinctly like it might be, yes, mustard yellow.

In the middle of an underwater graveyard, feet planted in the silt, a woman in an archaic high-pressure suit held an undulating white flag in her right hand. Her gaze canted left; a jellyfish hovered behind her. The overhanging veil of night suffused the scene made for a woebegone scene.

'Lovely!' rejoiced Alban Wouters.

The gallery owner stood and studied the bristol paper from afar, the better to take in the whole. Then he called Renée to hold the work against a bare wall.

'A black frame, I think,' said Alban Wouters, ecstatic.

'No, white,' his employee demurred. 'The drawing's already dark. A margin would add a double border.'

Sarah-Jeanne Loubier, ever silent, stared at Alban Wouters staring at her drawing. A sliver of a smile was forming on the left side of his mouth.

'Good,' he said. 'White it is. Don't forget to call the framer this afternoon, please.'

Alban Wouters noted that it was already noon, and would the artist like to eat? Sarah-Jeanne Loubier raised no objections, and they set forth with a nod to Renée, who would be left as ever to hold down the fort. Before leaving, Sarah-Jeanne Loubier took a final glance at the gallery walls and called up a furtive vision of her drawing hung there before a crowd of unknown people, multiplied by her imagination, one of whom might even purchase it at what still seemed to her an outlandish price. This vision filled Sarah-Jeanne with a sense of contentment far deeper than mere selfish regard, more akin to a heightening of self-knowledge coupled with an exponential increase in her power over her innermost self. This insight struck her as a seismic shift: of late she had caught people treating her with a respect she'd never known, if for *people* we read *adults*. She had, in short, gained ingress into *the adult world.*

There was no room at the Café des Éditeurs, so they went across the street to the Blue Dog. Before Sarah-Jeanne had time to even scan the menu, Alban Wouters let her know it would of course be his treat. Sarah-Jeanne hoped she might repay the favour one day.

'I'm leaning toward the shrimp tagliatelle,' he said. 'You?'

'I've been dreaming of a good steak-frites!'

'As have I, as have I,' Alban Wouters concurred. 'But my arteries see things differently. That's what happens when we get older. Ahh, time. I have a confession to make. You know, you've got me thinking. Because of you – or rather, thanks to you – I realize I no longer quite have my finger on the pulse. I'm out of touch with your generation. I mean, sure, I have the pleasure of mingling, from time to time, with young people, people your age. Yet you remain a mystery to me.'

The server appeared, took their order, recommended a Ripasso, and discreetly disappeared. A detail leapt to Alban Wouters's attention: Sarah-Jeanne Loubier's eyes were once again visible, as if back from a period of hibernation, a miracle explained by the fact that the chestnut bangs that covered them had since their last meeting been pruned by a skilled practitioner of the tonsorial arts, yet this transformation seemed to bespeak a renewal tantamount to the arrival of a springtime in her innermost heart of hearts.

Sarah-Jeanne was a changed woman. Two weeks ago, she had shed her boyfriend (of whom our narrative has made no mention up to now, as befits his utter insignificance). He was the kind of person prey to tortuous bouts of jealousy directed not at the hypothetical male lying in wait to snatch away his beautiful one but, infinitely more cruel, at the formidable talent of Sarah-Jeanne Loubier herself, whose success would always outshine his own. This cad was envious of the admiration she excited from every quarter and of the acclaim she garnered from tastemakers and scenesters. Sarah-Jeanne had lugged this jealousy behind her like a dead weight long enough. She had not broken free without a struggle, but, driven by a survival instinct whose purpose had been for a time unclear but had recently come back into sharp focus: a newfound freedom had exponentially multiplied the powers of Sarah-Jeanne Loubier.

Without even a hint of segue, Alban Wouters moved on to describe how in his younger days he'd been a fixture at all the best little galleries, biennials, and student shows; he'd been there, done that, taken notes. A keen student of art history, Alban had put a considerable dent in his savings with the acquisition of a few inexpensive works, certain of which had skyrocketed in value in a mere two years – notably three collages by a young, not overly prolific artist whose standing was buoyed up by untimely death – and Alban Wouters soon grasped how the game of speculation was played. He'd shown a certain flair. After a few early successes, he'd cast aside his dream of being an art historian and found a space for lease downtown, where he set up the shop he'd happily run ever since. And business hummed along, purring like a limousine engine, though purring can never be a perpetual state in a business whose product, by its very nature, must fall out of fashion. That's just the way it is. No work is impervious to the years; they are, like us, subject to the changing epochs and prey to the vagaries of time – which never passes without exacting a toll of fatigue on the Works of Men (and of Women, noted Sarah-Jeanne Loubier in her mental appendix). But what can you do? Years passed. Until the day, Alban Wouters continued, when, as you clearly see, we find ourselves, if not quite with our fingers no longer on the pulse, at best standing on the sidelines, watching, as a new generation comes on the scene, followed by another, still newer one, and aware that, while up to now you'd been content to follow the youth from a distance, you now regret to see that stupidly – and inexorably – you have really and truly lost touch. But such is life, no?

'I guess I've begun getting old but managed to avoid becoming nostalgic,' Alban Wouters congratulated himself. (Old, check, but you forgot 'windbag,' noted Sarah-Jeanne Loubier in the margin.) 'But still, I'm a businessman, and it's not in my interest to lose touch with what's happening.'

What the gallery owner was after – the point to which he was at very long last mercifully coming – was his need of an associate, someone to frequent on his behalf that vital circuit of happenings and little galleries. A young person – not too young, mind you – someone who had the eye, and a certain flair, and three other fully functional senses as well.

It was at that precise moment that a man bolted, with scant regard for vehicular traffic, across the busy street that harboured the Blue Dog. Sarah-Jeanne, interest piqued by the sight, was treated to the climax of the spectacle, set to a crescendoing soundtrack of car horns. The leading man was none other than her drawing teacher.

She saw Pierre-Luc running frantically, with no clear sense of why, or after whom. But his appearance gave her a brainwave and she leapt up.

'Excuse me a second,' she pleaded. 'There's someone I'd like you to meet.'

It's not like anyone's ever asked, but if you want my definition of art, here it is: *art is work for work's sake.* I know my axiom may come as a shock to certain artists who've never looked beyond the strictly utilitarian sense of the word *work.* But I stand behind my assertion: work for work's sake is the only work free of utility. And art is no less than the subversion of work. Others will object: my definition is too broad, it encompasses classes of artisans no one has ever deigned to think of as artists, not to mention the armies of upstanding folk who hold work sacred and would do it whether they were paid or not. With my deep-seated love of my métier, this is a category in which I must include myself. Does that mean that anyone at all can be an artist? I actually consider my definition quite restrictive. It excludes the great many people who call themselves artists but are driven by mercenary concerns, or do whatever happens to be fashionable, or whatever sells, or whatever makes them popular. Such work is excluded prima facie: its aim is not work, ergo it is not art. I'm fully aware that my definition of art – a definition whose elegance I hold to be irreproachable – is sure to raise controversy. But what can I do? I am no theorist; academe has never been my calling. It's not my business to convince anyone of anything. I can only admit what a great relief it is to me that all these things are finally said.

Now let's cue our story back up and join Pierre-Luc at the exact moment when the individual in a leather jacket and black glasses stole the camera he had used to capture the inside of Melanco's clandestine office from a range of angles.

Before the initial shock could wear off, Pierre-Luc had already set off in pursuit of the thief who had swiped the superzoom camera whose purchase had made such inroads into his already tight budget. A stroke of luck: the robber tripped on a paving stone in the Grand Square. A counterstroke: Pierre-Luc caught his foot on the very same paving stone, and the fleeing pillager got back his head start.

Pierre-Luc had strong legs. Though his right arm was still unusable, the new vocation he had found since being released from hospital had given him occasion to walk great distances.

At the bottom of it all was Célestine. It was she who had told Pierre-Luc all about the coup d'état led by Subcommander Sorgue, and about Faya's obscure connection to these at least geographically distant events.

Célestine wasn't at liberty to tell him everything, of course – state secrets must be kept secret. She simply explained that the authorities' hands were tied for now, *diplomatie oblige*, slipped an address into Pierre-Luc's hand, and asked whether he might be available for a task that required the utmost discretion.

And so he found himself before an aristocratic apartment, which he decided to reconnoitre from the café across the street where outrageously priced espresso was served alongside disdainful biscotti. A few hours later a ropy man emerged from the apartment and walked straight to the end of the street, where he climbed into a brand-new Anderloni. Pierre-Luc, who followed the suspect at a distance, hailed a taxi, a species thick on the ground mid-afternoon.

'Follow the red car,' he said.

Catching up with the vehicle in question wasn't difficult, as its progress was slowed, like everyone else's, by intersections and roundabouts. They left downtown. Before long, the Anderloni parked near the entrance to the Franchepart Woods, a sprawling park where at this afternoon hour idle women walked dogs and severed ties with tiresome lovers. Pierre-Luc asked the driver to drop him off a little farther, in order (he hoped) to dispel suspicion. He left a big tip and set off for the park gate.

The ropy man was advancing with a determined step. Clearly a meeting was afoot, a fact Pierre-Luc was able to confirm after a few zigzags through the tired plane trees. In front of a fountain in the distance, a tall Black man with a pelisse under his arm stood waiting. Pierre-Luc entertained vague thoughts of the Port Merveille insurgents. From his position, he couldn't really figure out what these two men were talking about; what was clear was that cutthroat negotiations were underway. What was that? Did he hear the word *diamond?* Let's not get carried away.

The men separated without so much as a handshake. Each set off in an opposite direction, and for a fraction of a second Pierre-Luc didn't know who to follow. He opted for the tall Black man.

He was mentally prepared for another pursuit by taxi. But this stranger preferred public transit: he joined the line of people watching for a tram next to the park gate. Pierre-Luc quickly withdrew behind the fence and pretended to wait for someone, a subterfuge achieved by means of regular theatrical glances at a non-existent watch. At last the tram appeared; Pierre-Luc waited for everyone to pack in and ran up at the last minute. The car was crowded, but the pursuer quickly caught sight of his mark, whose head stood helpfully a few centimetres above the crowd. Funny: he felt as though he recognized the man. He'd seen him before somewhere, or at any rate someone who looked a lot like him. The closing night of Simone's show, a man she'd spoken to at length ... but that was impossible, the world wasn't that small.

The chase was complicated by an impromptu transfer at Place du Midi. The next tram was on time; people packed in again, as crowds of employees got on after their workdays. Pierre-Luc was grateful that his subject seemed not to have noticed his existence.

At Gare de Sienne, the Black man got off suddenly; Pierre-Luc pretended to realize he'd reached his station in the nick of time. He then followed his mark to Platform 12, where the train to Collinges-les-Eaux stood waiting; Pierre-Luc thought fast, ran to the ticket office, lined up with nervous looks at the platform. He silently tapped his foot, studying each reconfiguration of the departures board in the hope of an unforeseen delay for the train at

Platform 12. An impassive final call rang through the boundless station, and the train left at the very moment when Pierre-Luc finally held a ticket in his hand.

This failure to complete his mission felt to Pierre-Luc like a grave disappointment; he began questioning his own abilities and along with them his chances of ever finding Faya. He walked out of the station, wandered a few minutes along the sidewalk, then looked up and walked into a café. He sat at the bar and ordered a toasted white-cheese sandwich and a beer, which he held in his right hand (his left still immobilized by a cast). That's when Debruyn and I came in, settled next to him, and bid the waiter bring us the same. I gave Pierre-Luc a friendly clap on the back and rhetorically asked what the matter was. Debruyn devoured his toasted cheese in a few mouthfuls. Pierre-Luc wasn't normally one to talk to strangers, but I broke the ice by chatting about art (a newspaper lay open on the bar to a story about the Fauret museum renovations, giving me pretext to steer our talk in that direction). Pierre-Luc admitted he had never given much thought to his personal definition of art, if he had one at all, which to be honest was astonishing, given that he had once been an artist and even a teacher of drawing.

Leafing distractedly through the newspaper, I fell upon the international news and pretended to only now notice a short article about the Port Merveille coup.

'Now there's a subject,' I said, 'that's of great interest to us, of very great interest indeed, isn't that right, Debruyn,' I said to Debruyn as he scarfed down my cheese sandwich. Pierre-Luc, surprised, replied that he only followed the news a little, but had heard something. 'It's all about diamonds,' I said, abruptly and without transition, 'nothing to do with the people's well-being. Or at least that's what they say at the ministry, isn't it, Debruyn? There are plenty of people at the ministry who'd like to know just what sort of scheme Subcommander Sorgue is hatching. Isn't that right, Debruyn?'

After subtly sounding the man out, I drained my beer and left a bill on the counter, with a gesture to inform the waiter that it would cover the three beers and three toasted white-cheese sandwiches. Finally, with a look meant to suggest I was acting on a sudden impulse, I held out a card to Pierre-Luc, who didn't know what to stammer back. 'Just in case,' I said, smiling, before leaving the premises with a hasty goodbye (while Debruyn slipped out without fanfare).

So it was that, a few days later, adequately but not overly informed by a briefing we arranged, Pierre-Luc abandoned his pursuit of Émilien Surville and found himself at the Grand Square, happily passing as a tourist who had chosen not to call off his trip because of a mere accident, an amateur photographer who must have loved brutalist architecture, indeed, to so exhaustively document the poor green building that seemed to offer little to attract such keen interest but in fact housed the secret offices of Melanco.

To what use would these shots be put? Pierre-Luc had no idea; nor would he learn anything further, since the photos, as well as the camera and the man who had stolen it, were now on the point of slipping definitively from his grasp.

So it was that after abruptly crossing the busy street (exactly adjacent to the Blue Dog, where the gallery owner was eating lunch with a young artist), the thief had absconded into an alley that dead-ended at a rather high wall. Luck is on my side, thought the breathless Pierre-Luc.

But no: with cheeky ease, the rogue was already climbing onto a garbage can and preparing to clear the obstacle. Our exhausted hero wanted to keep him on the near side of the wall, and to this end had snagged his fingers onto the right back pocket of his trousers. The seam ripped and the villain disappeared from view completely.

At which point the helpful Sarah-Jeanne Loubier appeared.

'What are you doing on the ground?' she asked. 'And what's up with that cast? Did you break your arm?'

Uncertain how much of his new occupation he was at liberty to reveal, Pierre-Luc said only that his superzoom camera had been stolen by the man who had just given him the slip.

Sarah-Jeanne Loubier interpreted this latest news as a sign that her former teacher was still unemployed. She was on the verge of inviting him to the Blue Dog, where it would be her pleasure to introduce him to a potential employer, when she caught sight of something lying near the garbage can's broken lid: a magnetic card.

'You dropped something,' she said, picking it up.

'It's not mine,' said Pierre-Luc, to whom she had handed the object, emblazoned with the logo of a well-known hotel chain.

'Maybe a clue?' Sarah-Jeanne Loubier guessed. 'The thief.'

'Good lord!' Pierre-Luc exclaimed. 'The card must have been in the back pocket of his pants. The back pocket ripped off, so of course the card fell out. What luck!'

They took a closer look at the magnetic card. Without a doubt, a door somewhere was waiting for this card to spring its lock.

'Look, on the back. *No. 206*,' said Sarah-Jeanne.

There are two types of existential angst, Simone informed Charles Rose: there's angst before the void, and angst in the face of excess. The former is the stronger of the two, setting us on a never-ending course of self-invention to keep us from the slough of despond, where we sink as into quicksand. The other type stems from a surfeit of ego, an excess of all that has led up to our own existence – the places we've lived, the people we've met. This second kind of angst leads to an excess in the humours that can be expelled much as you blow your nose, if you'll allow the metaphor; with the appropriate effort it can, in a manner of speaking, be shaken loose. Paradoxically, the two forms of angst can coexist. One can provide a premise for the other, and vice versa. The thing is, Simone said, we're constructions of stories and places, and our entire understanding of the world depends in large part on the subject of these stories and these places, what they reveal, what they withhold. Because sometimes stories and places cease to speak to us, and we may imagine that they're dead to us, and that must be because they are indeed dead to us.

The night before, Simone and Charles Rose had gone to a movie about a simple young man condemned to invent stories in order, he claimed, to invent himself. These stories hung by the most tenuous of threads, forever threatening to snap, and they advanced to their conclusion via the most circuitous of paths, leaving us with at best a jury-rigged ending, while the next story was already taking shape. The man in the film, if memory serves, was a clerical employee, living somewhere in the suburbs of a capital city in the New World. It all felt like a fable, but obviously wasn't.

Charles Rose brought coffee. He wasn't dressed, and Simone, under blankets rumpled by the night, was happy to welcome him as he was. Charles Rose loved waking up in Simone's room, among her fabrics and her papers. The early-rising sun formed blurry-edged patterns dancing on the wall. The closet mirror showed Charles Rose the endearing image of their mismatched bodies, so different yet so proximate. Simone, leaning against the headboard, slowly drank her coffee. This time tomorrow they'd be lawfully wedded.

No idea brought Charles Rose more pleasure than the thought of this unexpected marriage. There remained this matter of the diamond to attend to, and then ... it would be goodbye to the Service, goodbye to these overwrought dramas. He was certain he'd never loved anyone the way he loved Simone, with a love that grew stronger every day. He loved the way she seemed to have lived a thousand lives before this one, and he loved arriving in her life after so many others, being one more on her list, neither superseding those who'd come before nor the next logical rung in the succession they'd initiated. No, this love story had simply happened, without rhyme or reason.

Simone's look met his in the closet mirror, a serious look that came with a serious smile. The morning was warm.

'Do we always,' she pondered, 'see ourselves as reflected in a mirror?'

Charles Rose turned his head; Simone didn't move. He was affected by the sight of her skin, so tender from every angle. He bit her shoulder, kissed the nape of her neck. And then the lovers kissed full on the mouth, torrentially.

Charles Rose finished crafting his Eldredge knot and went down to the kitchen. Simone was in a robe, slicing bread. It seemed preposterous that Charles Rose should have to run an errand in town, especially after a morning like that one, particularly on their wedding day. But there you had it. He had things to settle for work. First a stop at the bank, then the embassy, and then ... So many obligations. His had always been a life governed by all manner of obligations. And yet it was precisely these obligations that had led to his meeting with Simone. And today he was finally ready to give a violent kick to the scaffolding that had supported him through the lead-up to this delightful next chapter in his story.

He called a cab. Then he kissed Simone one more time and slid warm hands under her dress while she caressed the thing growing hard in his pants. That night, that night, they promised.

A day of fierce beauty. Fresh air streamed through the open window, caressing Charles Rose's joyful face. The taxi dropped him off at the travel agency. He picked up his train tickets. 'For my honeymoon,' he informed the ticket seller. 'No one gets married anymore,' she opined. Luckily, Charles Rose had no fear of anachronism.

He slid his tickets into the pocket of his pelisse and decided to walk to the bank since it was such a lovely day. He calmly crossed the boulevard and slipped into an ill-lit covered passage that made a useful shortcut, unknown even to some neighbourhood residents. Half the storefronts in the passageway stood empty; the others languished behind a layer of dust. If he were rich, Charles Rose would have bought the entire arcade, set up an office, opened a gallery. He stopped. Windows and doors were elaborately framed, mosaics shy a tile or two enlivened the poorly maintained sidewalk. Spent light bulbs had long given up any hope of being replaced. Behind one grimy window he intuited a philatelist's; another seemed to house a moribund barbershop, the next door over advertised the services of a notary public and commissioner of oaths. One window's faded paint afforded a glimpse into a café abandoned post-haste as the bombs of some long-past world war began to fall.

Of course, no such passage would be complete without a bookseller with a shock of white hair, ensconced amid stacks of insipid esoterica. His establishment was the sole outpost that yet welcomed the few spectres still haunting what must once have been a bustling place of commerce. Finding himself observed, the bookseller raised a reproving glance at Charles Rose, who at that very moment felt a thud in the back of the neck, and then nothing at all.

Charles Rose, or Fabrice Mansaré, or whatever name you choose to call him by (there must be more), was blessed with a rich inner life. And one part of this inner life was buried in the deepest strata of his subconscious, where its heart still beat and whence some part of it sometimes, under intense mental pressure, was forced to the surface with an ominous black light.

A beautiful blond woman came into Fabrice Mansaré's still-hazy field of vision. He stirred; unfruitful movements indicated that he was tied to a chair, as was to be expected. The woman approached. Hadn't he seen her somewhere before? His head hurt.

'Let's not beat around the bush, Mr. Mansaré. There's no point playing the tough guy,' said the woman. 'We know who you work for.'

Fabrice Mansaré was in a tight spot. It was certainly conceivable that information of that nature might have fallen into the hands of one of his enemies. But it was also the case that he worked for a great many different people, not all of whom were necessarily acquainted. One thing was sure: he knew how to shut up. Still dazed, he mentally reviewed his mission notes. Who could have kidnapped him like this?

'Let's cut to the chase,' the tall blonde suggested. 'Where's the Supreme Orchestra?'

The diamond. But that wasn't of much help to Fabrice Mansaré. A lot of people wanted the Supreme Orchestra. Not all for the same reasons.

They were at the centre of an unoccupied floor of a building whose ceilings seemed to go on forever, striped with buzzing fluorescent tubes, probably the erstwhile offices of some concern whose cubicles had been put out to pasture. Fabrice Mansaré guessed there would be individuals in lab coats observing him from behind the one-way mirrors of the closed offices that surrounded this large bare room – bare, that is, save for the turned-off TV that loomed atop a grey metal cabinet, plugged into a series of blue extension cords.

Along with these observations, Fabrice Mansaré's mind was coursing with the information the Service had provided during their instructive rides in the back seats of black sedans with tinted windows. He recalled the mention of Problem 30, a Melanco secret agent whose presence in Bruant had set the brass's nerves on edge. Everything was coming clear.

'You're planning to play a dirty trick on your father,' said Problem 30, smiling like a hyena (I say this in full knowledge that the hyena's smile expresses nothing that can be properly associated with human emotions).

Fabrice Mansaré's silence in no way reflected mental inaction. An unpleasant moment, something to get through, he repeated to himself. These people couldn't hold him here forever, the higher-ups would worry, there'd be repercussions … Nor could they kill him: only he knew the code to the safety deposit box where the Supreme Orchestra was stored. Perhaps there was something more serious he was missing. Problem 30 turned on the TV.

'Speaking of family,' she said.

A blurry image took form: the live feed of a surveillance camera, as evinced by the running time-stamp on the bottom of the screen. At the centre of the image was an unmade bed flanked by little night tables, the usual trappings of a cheap hotel room.

'Don't think it was easy to find her,' Problem 30 continued. 'But as you can see we've gone to great lengths to make you happy. We know you've never had the pleasure of meeting Eugénie, your sister's daughter. Well, here she is.'

Fabrice Mansaré strained his eyes but couldn't make out a human figure on the screen. What game were they playing? Then he saw: a young woman with kinky hair appeared in the camera's field of vision, fell onto the unmade bed, and collapsed, as if weighted down by a great lassitude. She didn't appear to have been mistreated. Drugged? But it was Eugénie, he was certain of it. Fabrice Mansaré almost fainted. It was his niece, without a doubt. She must be twenty-eight, give or take. A powerful emotion overcame him, which soon took on an unsavoury cast. His sister's daughter … the daughter of …

'What do you want from me?' yelled Fabrice Mansaré, shaking in the chair to which he remained bound.

'The diamond, Mr. Mansaré, the diamond. Look, we don't enjoy resorting to such extreme measures any more than you do. But the stability of the entire region is at stake.'

Sweat poured down Fabrice Mansaré's forehead. He couldn't take his eyes off the screen. He suppressed the vision that had leapt into his mind, a fallout shelter; only hypnosis, or some other truth-extracting procedure, could have brought it to light. No. Nothing had happened in that shelter. Nothing beyond what was without a doubt a somewhat cruel episode of privation orchestrated by General Mansaré to show his son what he was really worth. The first chapter of his martial education, after which, for reasons that eluded him, he and his sister had been separated. And if, after all these years, he'd never attempted to see her, it must be because … In the end, there was no need to go searching for an answer. And as for his at best ambivalent feelings about his father …

This psychological bouillabaisse certainly warranted its own in-depth analysis, but not from the likes of us, mere dilettantes who have read a book or two. Even we can see that the sight of Eugénie had thrown Fabrice Mansaré into a state of profound shock. The gorgeous blonde, who had been counting on just this mental insta-bility, cackled heartily.

'Why waste our energy on all this talk of diamonds. What would you say if I filled you in on certain details that concern you, that in fact concern you *very intimately?* Things you are, quite clearly, *unaware of.*'

In a final effort to defend himself, Fabrice Mansaré nudged his train of thought back onto the track that led to Simone. This manoeuvre enabled him to get hold of himself. Soon he was no longer hearing his antagonist. He was in the gallery, on the day of the exhibition closing, where he met for the first time that astonishing woman with ash-blond hair and prominent cheekbones, an artist with a rich and conflicted mental landscape, a tender and delicate mistress with a boundless imagination. His wife-to-be. Champagne flute in hand, he congratulated her on the exhibition, asked what had led her to erotic drawing; she answered that it had happened quite by chance: she had a way of setting people at ease, why or how she could not say, and then so many people were looking for just such a medium whereby they might expose themselves without compromise, so in a sense she was merely a catalyst, and Simone had to admit she derived great pleasure from the exercise, nor could she say whether this pleasure was something she took from her models, or rather some gratuitous dividend, a magical surplus. Building on this idea, they struck up a lively conversation on theories of expenditure and the nature of gifts, a conversation that proved to have legs. Finally Fabrice Mansaré introduced himself as Charles Rose, and followed this by asking whether she might grant him the pleasure of taking him as a model. The proposition might easily have importuned Simone, who surely didn't work with just anyone. But she didn't turn him down. He may have suddenly found himself being presumptuous, but Simone had said yes.

Problem 30 was still speaking, but Fabrice Mansaré wasn't listening anymore. The episode in the gallery was not over yet; it was critical to draw it out further. What had happened after? Oh yes, the gallery owner had brought him the drawing of Simone's that he had purchased. 'Let me wrap it, it'll be more discreet that way,' joked the gallery owner. And Simone's curious reaction to his choice of work? 'Oh really, you chose that one?' 'It spoke to me,' Charles Rose admitted. 'I don't know why, but it spoke to me. There's a laid-back but powerful resistance in it. I don't know much about drawing, but I feel like you've invested a lot of yourself in it.' 'It's possible,' said Simone. 'I don't really ask myself questions when I'm drawing, you know, don't really want to think about all the parts of me that go into my work, unconsciously.' 'Who knows, maybe you unconsciously put something of me into your drawing,' said Charles Rose delicately. The conversation was leading him to to ask certain questions of himself as well.

And Fabrice Mansaré again saw the drawing, *Faya Sitting, 18/20*, which he had not yet, for no clear reason, got around to hanging on his living room wall, and which Simone, undoubtedly annoyed to see it still leaning against the wall in the hallway, had eventually put away in a drawer of the commode. A light bulb lit up.

'That's not Eugénie!' he said, leaping up to the extent permitted by his ropes.

And in effect, a close look at the girl on the television revealed that it was clearly Faya. Faya, whose drawing he knew all too well, and who he had seen in the flesh as well, in the gallery, the day of the closing. That was why she'd seemed so familiar. The rest had been mere suggestion. He found his courage. Still, it was weird how Faya … How that drawing … No matter, Faya wasn't his niece. Or anything else to him. And with that he slipped the most simplistic trap anyone had ever laid for him. Melanco was powerless against him. Now it was Fabrice Mansaré's turn to smile.

'That girl has nothing to do with your business,' he said. 'Let her go.'

Problem 30 stopped her monologue; she didn't immediately register the shift, she who had ably set this psychic snare. She had no further opportunity to think about it: on the screen, Faya was headed for the bedroom door, as if called by a voice, where she grasped the handle, which she suddenly yanked on with all her strength.

'It's no use,' said Problem 30, 'we've locked it from the outside.'

Yet against all expectations the door opened. A man came in, one we recognized thanks to the cast on his arm, who Faya knew and greeted with a kiss. Another woman followed him in, a student Problem 30 didn't recognize. Faya led them both out and left the room.

And Fabrice Mansaré, who finally had all his wits about him, finished untying the knots that bound him, coolly stood up, and informed his kidnappers he would be doing the same.

It was time to report in. Debruyn was waiting for me in the Cholet. My tardiness made him grumpy, but I had a 156-page report to print out.

The chief's office was a cube with faded walls hidden by overflowing shelves, in the middle of which sat a verdigris desk piled high with binders, hordes of folders, a diligently crossed-off weekly planner, a black Bakelite telephone, and a fake wood Rolodex, along with a massive grey terminal fed by reams of computer paper, serving as typewriter, all basking in the bluish gleam of an articulated metal lamp resting in its faithful stainless-steel socket. When we walked in, the chief was glumly looking over an internal manual whose glossy cover in garishly bright colours depicted actors of both sexes disguised as average employees, grinning improbably as they gathered around a shiny new computer. The chief beckoned us to sit. The leatherette chairs were seriously eroding.

'Oh boy,' said the chief who, after closing the manual, set down his glasses on the desk, the better to welcome us. 'Look at this, as if there wasn't enough to do … Now I'm supposed to "diversify the workforce,"' he complained. 'Do you guys realize what that means? Women! Hire women, and send them out into the field with you! It'll be mayhem!'

'C'mon,' protested Debruyn. 'No need to be sexist.'

I was silently grateful to Debruyn for making his stand. After all these years, it was as if the chief had forgotten that I was a woman.

'Well, that's the last straw. Maybe it's not a bad thing that I'll be retiring this year.'

I tossed out a 'We'll miss you,' to be nice.

'And so,' he said, coming to the business at hand. 'To the business at hand. Can you paint me a picture?'

'Of course,' I said, pulling from my bag a purple folder that Debruyn passed on to the chief. 'It's all in the report. Pretty straightforward, you'll see. First there was the dead body. Poulcq.'

'Poulcq,' he said, summoning the memory. 'Former Service.'

'Exactly,' I confirmed. 'At first we couldn't figure out what he was doing there. Freelancing? Moving on to another agency? It was hard to say for sure. But there was clearly a connection between his presence at Charles Rose's and the diamonds.'

'Remind me: what's the deal with the diamonds?' asked the chief, massaging his forehead. 'I'm a little lost.'

'Nothing fancy,' I offered. 'Diamond mining has been the main source of revenue for the autocratic regime of General Mansaré – and his puppet president, Chénier – since the overthrow of Koroboume, the last legitimate president of the former colony, now a republic. A regime change our own government backed, let's not forget,' I offered as background.

'In matters like this, it's best to spare no detail,' the chief encouraged me.

'And now,' I went on, 'General Mansaré is getting old, and all of Port Merveille is plotting to replace him. Some of the frontrunners are Subcommander Sorgue and his United Liberation Front, a left-leaning faction that wants to reinstate a democratic, progressive republic. The powers that be no longer have the resources to suppress the revolt, so they have to forge alliances. That's why General Mansaré sent his son out on a diplomatic mission.'

'All pretty standard,' noted the chief.

'And it has come to light, as you know, that Fabrice Mansaré, under the name Charles Rose, was already one of our many foreign operatives. And in this capacity he is called on to play a double role, since this time our government has secretly sided with the insurgents. The thing is that Charles Rose has ascertained that Sorgue is more than willing, in exchange for the right military and humanitarian aid, to lift certain export tariffs on precious stones and gems. Manna from heaven for the diamond traders who are the pride of our nation. As a token of good faith, we've even agreed to clandestinely send one of our leading intellectuals, who's sympathetic to their cause, to Port Merveille. Doesn't cost us a thing, helps build rapport.'

'Geopolitically expedient,' the chief congratulated us.

'The catch is that we're not alone. And Melanco – who I don't need to remind you are ready to fight tooth and nail for General Mansaré's government, their last bulwark against the scourge of socialism – has thrown a major problem our way. A *tall* problem,' I specified. 'A *tall* problem with *blond* hair.'

'You know your allusions are quite beyond me,' the chief scolded.

'Problem 30!' I spelled it out. 'Problem 30 has adopted the identity of one Célestine, singer of the pop group Poupée Sincère – you must have heard "Facing North."' (Here I hummed a few faltering but recognizable bars.) 'No? I'm surprised, it's all over the radio these last few weeks. Anyway, all this to say that Problem 30 has no intention of giving up until she has laid hands on the Supreme Orchestra – a pink diamond, 148 carats and change,' I added. 'And as it happens, through a stroke of good luck we may have time to tell you about another day, the Service has been fortunate enough to obtain this spectacular gemstone, which General Mansaré, with his back against the wall, secretly handed over to Melanco to inject some funds into his war coffers. Funds which, needless to say, have been slow to arrive, since the Supreme Orchestra is no longer in their possession, but rather in ours, or more precisely, Fabrice Mansaré's. And that's where Prince Ludwig comes in.'

'Hold your horses,' said the chief. 'What the hell does Prince Ludwig have to do with this?'

'Well, he has agents of his own, of course,' I informed my superior, 'including one Surville. But what's of interest to us is that the prince is quite the diamond lover. There's no price he won't pay to get a hold of the Supreme Orchestra. So, this Surville got in touch with Charles Rose, and they negotiated and agreed on a price, and they're going to seal the deal any day now. To be honest, it proved more complicated than expected. And all because of Charles Rose, or more precisely Charles Rose's fiancée, and more precisely still the mysterious friendship this Charles Rose's fiancée struck up with Princess Cécile.'

'I can feel the plot thickening,' the chief intuited, swallowing two ibuprofen.

'Let's just say that our operative's love life has thrown a few spanners in the works,' I admitted. 'But we felt the best course of action was not to come between them. You might say that the Service has always had a proclivity for imbroglio. But it is this very proclivity that has kept our nation safe and on course. So we're keeping an eye on the fiancée. One Simone, Simone Bergmann. Funnily enough, this Simone is no stranger to us. She showed up in our files, a fairly spectacular affair, over twenty years ago.'

'When I said "best to spare no detail,"' the chief pleaded with me, 'I meant there are perhaps a few we could save for another time.'

'Certainly,' I obliged him. 'But Simone comes with a full cast of new characters. To wit, one "Faya" – clearly a cryptonym – with whom she was intimate for some time, and who as it turns out hails from Port Merveille. Otherwise, nothing to do with our story. But Melanco must have seen an opportunity to take advantage of this coincidence and kidnap the young woman, passing her off as Eugénie Fliess, niece of Fabrice Mansaré – I'm sure you're still with me – who she does in fact greatly resemble. In the appendix to my report you'll find photographs. And here another character comes into play, one Pierre-Luc Montaigne. Also an associate of Simone's. Currently unemployed.'

'Is this really important?' asked the chief.

'A secondary plot line,' I admitted. 'Pierre-Luc came onto our radar quite by accident. Let's say he made a surprise visit onto the hood of our car, before being recruited – for purposes we've yet to fully ascertain – by Problem 30 herself, under her civilian identity, of course. She took it upon herself to send him on the trail of Faya, who had disappeared. A misleading trail that we righted as soon as we could. But, honestly, we still haven't quite figured out that entire episode … Anyway, what matters is that Pierre-Luc has been highly useful to us. I don't believe he fully understands just how useful …'

The chief stood up, the better to think.

'It's all crystal clear, yes,' he said. 'Classic, really. There's just one thing I don't quite get. This Charles Rose, a.k.a. Fabrice Mansaré, a.k.a. who knows what else … this agent of the many names, if you will. Correct me if I'm wrong, but we are asking him to act against the interests of his own father. How can we be sure he won't betray us? What are we to him?'

'The Service trusts him,' I clarified. 'In a sense, where his true allegiances lie is a matter of indifference to us. He has provided us valuable intel from Sorgue, and that's all we've asked of him. As for the Supreme Orchestra, all we have to do is keep an eye on what he does with the money once the transaction is complete. And when you get down to it,' I added innocently, 'what do I know of the depths of the human soul, of what could cause us to betray our origins, our family, our father. I'm just a humble artist.'

'Artist?'

'We're all artists,' I said, 'in our trade.'

As for the wedding, we weren't invited.

A grey morning hung over the Port of Bruant. A cool, salty sea breeze whistled through the opening in the taxi window. Fabrice Mansaré made sure he hadn't forgotten anything in the car, closed the door, and set off toward the docks with a small black case under his arm. He yawned. The wedding night had been wonderful. He checked to make sure the pocket of his pelisse still contained the train tickets. Simone was meeting him at the station very soon, and from there they'd catch the southbound express. To be on the safe side, he'd given Simone instructions for what to do if he didn't show up – or if he had company.

A few minutes passed. Fabrice Mansaré didn't like being exposed, out in the open on the docks. Just in case, he took up a position in the shadow of a deserted shack advertising tickets for a harbour cruise. You'd expect Surville to be more punctual. The abandoned buildings around the port made him ill at ease. A hundred metres out, an ocean liner idled. We could almost see the nearby harbour, with its yachts moored in neat rows. The minute hand on Fabrice Mansaré's watch crept forward from time to time. Gulls squabbled over the dregs of a paper cone of fries. This was unacceptable: they'd have to change the plan. Fabrice Mansaré walked calmly toward the Avenue du Port, tapping the pocket of his pelisse as if the train tickets might somehow have slipped out. Why would Surville stand him up? Had the prince changed his mind? Did he suspect something? Or was this just one more of Melanco's dirty tricks?

But no, the answer was straightforward: Surville was at the police station being interrogated about another matter altogether.

Very early that morning, two officers had knocked loudly on the door of his baronial suite, at the very moment when Émilien Surville was preparing to go meet Fabrice Mansaré, who was to hand over the diamond in exchange for two suitcases of hard currency. Their appearance at the precise moment when Émilien Surville was about to leave provoked a slight cognitive delay, as if he were suddenly some other person temporarily occupying his apartment.

But the policemen just asked gruffly if his name was Émilien Surville, and if he was indeed the owner of a mustard-yellow Anderloni that had gone missing two weeks earlier. Surville's heart was pounding. He was moved to hear that his car had been found, gutted to learn of the state it was in. What an outrage! Such a faithful machine, such exhilarating handling ... Still, the discovery did enable him to mourn with dignity. On the verge of tears, Émilien Surville put his hand on his chest and took a deep breath. He opened his eyes again; the police hadn't budged; their long faces had not shortened. 'Would you please come with us to the station now,' said one. Surville could protest to his heart's content, plead urgent business (the details of which he wasn't at liberty to discuss), offer to come by later, at their pleasure: nothing doing. The catch was that they'd found a body in the trunk of the vehicle, every bit as worse for wear as its conveyance, and relieved of its fingerprints to boot. Police forces do not look kindly on problems beyond their inductive capacities, and this distaste is transferred by osmosis to each of their members, as Surville found out soon enough, uncomfortably seated under an excessively bright light, peppered with indelicate questions concerning his whereabouts over the past few weeks. When they asked for the tenth time whether he was in the habit of driving around with a body in his trunk, he turned green with indignation and invoked the authority of Prince Ludwig, warning the officers that he had friends in Internal Affairs and that the embassy would not at all appreciate the way the police's treatment of one of their most illustrious nationals.

At that very moment, outraged exclamations could be heard approaching the interrogation room. The door opened to reveal an exceedingly contrite deputy minister, who rushed over to shake the hand of my dear Mr. Surville, and if you could please excuse this horrific misunderstanding, I only just found out, et cetera et cetera. On this note, the deputy-lieutenant who followed behind him indicated with an accusatory eyebrow that it was of the essence that they release their guest post-haste, and if they had any idea of the hot water they had put him in by picking up this stranger of noble birth and did they really believe people of this class got their kicks by driving their cars off cliffs with stiffs stuffed in the trunk? An outraged, bolt-upright Émilien Surville was showered in apologies by the deputy minister, who escorted him to the police station exit, and you can't take these brutes too seriously, they're just doing their job, we don't pay them to think, rest assured His Majesty the Prince can always count on me and on our government, and of course I understand your anger, Mr. Surville, what would you say to stopping by my place one of these days, I am truly humbled by your understanding and won't fail to mention it to the minister, who by the way sends warm regards. Surville finally broke away with a promise not to breathe a word to the prince, and added that this was clearly a misunderstanding of no importance and, when you got right down to it, everyone made mistakes sometimes.

Émilien Surville had completely missed his meeting. He looked at his watch: already eight-fifteen. What would the prince say when he failed to deliver the cherished rock?

Simone turned off the gas, closed the suitcases, locked the door, and waited in front of her house for the taxi. The night had been wonderful, albeit short, and she wasn't in the least cross with Charles Rose for reserving a sleeping car, expense be damned. She would, however, have preferred to ride to the station with her gentleman companion. To leave her husband's side the day after their wedding, even for a few hours, was simply not done. His business must be important. It would happily also be his last, if she were to believe her new husband's promises.

The road to the Gare du Midi was less congested than the highway to the airport; the taxi dropped her off a good half-hour early, at eight-thirty. Simone guided her suitcases to the top of the escalator and took an empty seat at the café, where she had coffee and a croissant while filling her sketchbook with likenesses of travellers, pigeons, and station workers.

Fabrice Mansaré had gone home to pick up his luggage. It was eight-fifteen when he finally got a call from Émilien Surville, who apologized for standing up his friend, claimed it was beyond his control, and grumbled something by the way about the uncouth manners of policemen. Fabrice Mansaré pretended he had no idea what the man was talking about. 'Listen,' Surville sputtered over the honking horns, 'let's put off our meeting until tomorrow, same time, same place.' 'Not possible,' snapped Fabrice Mansaré, 'I'm going on my honeymoon.' 'My associate will not be pleased,' Surville pleaded in a voice meant to be persuasive, with a hint of a threat. 'Well,' said Fabrice Mansaré, on whom the benefits of pushing up his drop-off were not lost, 'if your luggage is getting too heavy for you, I'd suggest the left luggage counter, Gare du Midi. There's a tailor across the street, Chez Octave. And I need a new shirt. Maybe you do too. I'll be there at 8:45. And make no mistake, I'll be gone at 8:46.'

Fabrice Mansaré hung up, switched to Plan B, and scribbled something on a scrap of paper that he then stuffed in his trouser pocket. He wet his face, pulled on a polo shirt, put on his sunglasses, picked up his suitcase, walked out of the apartment, and locked the door. Eschewing both the escalator and the lobby, he took the service stairs, four at a time, down to the parking level, then walked a good distance to the Boulevard des Anciennes Colonies. He was almost disappointed to find that this time there was no sedan with tinted windows waiting to scoop him up. He let a few taxis go by, flagging down the fourth that passed. 'Drive,' he ordered, before his ass settled on the seat, 'I'll tell you where to go.'

But the door to Fabrice Mansaré's apartment didn't stay locked for long: a gloved hand picked it expertly and three men in lab coats, followed by a tall woman, went unceremoniously into his living room. In silence, they opened drawers and books, turned over cushions and sheets, climbed under the bed and the couch, before finally uncovering a black case.

'Empty,' one of the laboratorians pronounced with the authority of an expert.

Problem 30 bit her lip.

'It's not too late,' she insisted.

At eight-forty-five, Émilien Surville came out of the left luggage office of the Gare du Midi. He slid into his pocket the small orbicular skeleton key, along with a receipt bearing the number of the compartment that now held, somewhat awkwardly, two black suitcases packed with nonsequential bills. Émilien Surville galloped without stopping past the café, failing to notice the person sitting there who in recent weeks had so confounded his intelligence. Simone, attentive behind her sketchbook, made a quick drawing of the clumsy man whose pestering conversation at the embassy ball she unhappily remembered.

Octave the tailor did brisk business. The small shop's location directly across from the station afforded it ample opportunity to come to the rescue of men who were left rumpled by a night spent on a train or in an ironless hotel room. They also did alterations. Émilien Surville's watch showed 8:43 when he hurriedly passed through the doorway. He saw Fabrice Mansaré at the back of the shop, comparing a pink shirt with an Italian collar to another, purple in colour. Surville caught his breath and said a friendly hello to the clerk (not Octave himself), explaining with a phony smile that he was just looking. The other customers in the boutique, a pair of tall men in long gabardine raincoats, also didn't seem to require the clerk's assistance.

Adjusting the knot on his tie, Émilien Surville pretended to peruse the merchandise on offer, then took a long hard look at an orange cardigan that couldn't have been less his style. 'The key,' Fabrice Mansaré, whose back was to him, whispered without interrupting his studies in chromatics. Surville nervously rummaged through his pocket and removed the key to the storage locker and the receipt thereto, and placed them on a pile of vests. Though far from adroit in this kind of manoeuvre, he nonetheless managed to pull it off without being seen and felt a fleeting blush of pride. The two men traded places. Surville studied the purple shirt that had been left on the rack; Fabrice Mansaré, who had settled on the pink, strode off toward the register.

Émilien Surville poked around at the purple shirt, nervously eyeing the two other gabardine-clad customers. He had a nagging feeling they were watching him. Under the fold of the collar he discovered the key to Fabrice Mansaré's apartment.

Under another he was poised to locate a piece of paper that promised to reveal the hiding spot, in the self-same apartment, of the Supreme Orchestra. At least, it would have had not a thick fist emerged behind him and grasped the hand holding the key, while the end of a silencer tickled his brachial plexus.

Then everything happened at once.

From our observation post on the mezzanine, we saw three men running toward the front door of the station. General Mansaré's henchmen, dressed in gabardine with pistols drawn, were chasing a third, the son of the leader himself, who held in his left hand an overnight bag and a plastic bag from a nearby menswear shop.

The three men had left behind, to bleed out on the tiles of the same boutique, the heroic cadaver of Émilien Surville, whose dying words, to his astonishment, were 'Long live the prince!'

Fabrice Mansaré, impeccably trained, swiftly carved a path through the crowd to the station entrance. He reached the foot of the escalators. Muffled by the deceitful silencer, the shots escaped his hearing, which registered only the breaking of glass and fearful shouts of innocent onlookers. He was halfway up the escalator when he felt a searing pain in his lower back. He paused a moment. His right hand felt the wound, pain radiating through his body, and he wondered if he'd ever make it to the top.

One of the shooters, who had also reached the bottom of the escalator, hit upon the bright idea of pressing the emergency stop button. The sudden halt caused Fabrice Mansaré to stumble.

The other assailant was already climbing toward him. With eyes only for his prey, he failed to see Debruyn who, straddling the concurrent escalator, knocked him out with a revolver. The villain somersaulted down the escalator backwards.

His associate, suddenly single-handed, momentarily forgot all about Fabrice Mansaré, who was painfully attempting to climb the immobilized stairs, and had the execrable idea of turning his gun on Debruyn, who hadn't taken sufficient care: he caught three slugs right in the gut. 'Debruyn!' I cried out when I saw my incredulous comrade go down. Without a moment's thought, I ran over and emptied my magazine into the assassin, who collapsed in a shower of blood.

'Debruyn! Good old Debruyn! It can't be!'

Charles Rose was startled to make it to the top of the escalator still standing, even more so to be greeted there by Simone who, having guessed that her new husband must be in the centre of the melee, had thrown caution to the wind and hastened to the scene of the drama.

'Let's go,' panted Charles Rose.

Simone held him up as they waddled toward the departures area. Lulled by the silence that descended after chaos, travellers made way for them, unaware of what had just happened. Police sirens ululated in the distance.

'You can't take the train like that,' Simone whispered.

Charles Rose, whose left side was reddening at a nasty pace, agreed.

'The washroom,' he gasped. 'I'll make a tourniquet.'

The crowd was only now seized with panic. Even those who hadn't seen or heard anything were looking for an exit. Simone helped Charles Rose press forward against the current; they reached the bathrooms and went in. They were alone. Charles Rose pushed open the door of a stall and lowered himself onto the toilet seat. His blood dripped onto the cold brown tile. Simone unbuttoned his stained shirt and took it off as gently as possible. What she saw wasn't pretty. She quickly unrolled the toilet paper and staunched as best she could the blood already drying around his loins, and discovered the wound, over which she placed a fresh but temporary gauze of toilet paper, battened in place with the sleeves of the stained shirt. She guessed a bullet must still be lodged in the wound.

Charles Rose was sweating profusely.

'Are you cold?' she asked.

He shook his head.

'The key,' he panted. He opened the bloody palm containing the skeleton key. She took it. Then he looked her in the eye.

'The left luggage,' he added.

'Charles,' she said sweetly, 'we'll have our honeymoon another time. Right?' She got up.

'Where are you going?' he panted.

'To the infirmary. You need help. It's just next door. I won't be gone a minute.'

She smiled sadly. He tried to return her smile. It came out as a grimace. He gestured in the direction of Simone's purse.

'Don't forget your,' he murmured.

Simone gave him one last look, suffused with affection. The mezzanine was deserted. She scanned it for a red cross on a white background. Her sight was growing dim. She felt dizzy. There was blood everywhere, covering Simone's hands, and cheeks, and blouse. Her eyes picked out the abandoned information kiosk; for a second she lost herself in the contemplation of a giant white question mark. Snapping her head back, she saw three men in lab coats going into the men's washroom. A tall blonde woman followed close behind, a gorgeous blonde who looked like she belonged in another world and was also the spitting image of the singer of Poupée Sincère. Simone thought of Faya again. The bathroom door was yanked open, and the laboratorians left. Behind them Célestine screamed.

'It's her! She's got the key!'

And Simone took a Browning from her handbag.

Her aim was true: four shots was all it took. Like bowling pins, the laboratorians fell one after another, united in their stupefaction.

Célestine didn't go down immediately. There was the sound of an engine backfire, then several bright flashes at the level of her chest. She raised her arm; sparks flew all around her shoulder. A small yellow flame rose up where her heart was lodged. She began blinking furiously. Finally she started singing:

Facing north, I play dead
Facing north, I play dead
Facing north, I play dead
Facing north, I play dead

SARAH-JEANNE AND PIERRE-LUC

Under a cloudless sky, deplaning passengers hit a wall of choking heat that the jet engines seemed to compound but in fact only palely imitated, a consubstantial heat that abated only when the terminal's air conditioning slapped you in the face.

The new Port Merveille International Airport was a sprawling construction site, put into service before it was completed. Travellers and workers shared the space with irrepressible gaiety, actors in and witnesses to the building of the modernist masterpiece that would make the entire world see the miracle that was the Democratic Republic, less than a year after its triumphant restoration.

With two heavy suitcases in tow, Pierre-Luc found Sarah-Jeanne Loubier waiting under the intrepid arches of the loading zone. Just beyond the taxi stand, she had spied a man in a white fitted suit that wasn't entirely up to the task of containing a pink-and-purple-patterned shirt, leaning casually against a seven-seater van, holding a piece of cardboard with their names.

They walked over. The man made a deeply satisfied gesture, stowed their luggage in the already full back, and invited them to get in. Two passengers were already seated inside.

Catching a cab at the airport is always more or less the same story, only somewhat different perhaps when you're in an unfamiliar land. To the eyes of our tourists, everything seemed incredibly mysterious, even the ordinariness of a highway so new the asphalt seemed still wet, as they sped unhindered by traffic through the heart of the bush. The silhouette of Port Merveille appeared behind a transparent veil of heat, a vision that evaporated completely the moment the driver veered onto a secondary road leading into the countryside.

After a few kilometres, they stopped on the edge of a vaguely delineated village square to let out an insurance salesman in a black flowing boubou returning home after a lengthy conference, but not without a quick stop in his mother's village, to deliver a large set of multicoloured plastic tubs. The driver politely let them take their time to finish the requisite exchange of news concerning their entire extended family down to each third and fourth cousin. When the time finally came for the insurance man to say his goodbye, a woman bearing on her head a sack of rice, and atop the sack, a gourd, appeared in the main square. A baby was strapped to her back; she was also accompanied by a young girl in a tank top, with a green pagne wrapped around her waist and a doll in her hand. The driver waited for them, got out, arranged the five floppy kilograms of rice between two suitcases. The woman insisted on holding the gourd between her knees. They got back on the road, which was now more of a track, an orange streak bisecting a yellow expanse randomly bordered by trees, shacks, and goats. The young girl soon overcame her shyness and introduced her doll to the peach-coloured strangers who shared her seat.

'Her name is Doualé.'

'Doualé, like your president,' said Sarah-Jeanne Loubier.

'She's the doll president!' said the proud girl as she took Sarah-Jeanne Loubier's hand.

The woman with the gourd sat behind them and watched the landscape go by, chewing on a miswak stick, as the baby on her back sucked an arrowroot candy. On the national radio station, the news was all good; the driver celebrated the resumption of the music with an enthusiastic adjustment to the volume level.

Two or three detours later, the seven-seater stopped before a yellow two-storey colonial villa with blue shutters, in front of which three palm trees stood in a line, the last serving as a stand for a yellow scooter. Simone appeared at the main door the instant the suitcases hit the floor. She joked with the driver, pulled a few bills from her pocket, handed them over, and said hello again. Then she tenderly kissed her two friends.

'It's so great to see you!'

Simone was tanned. Her ash-coloured hair was full of sparkles. She invited them in, assigned them a room, enjoined them to change, explained how the shower worked. 'Make yourself at home,' she said. 'I'll meet you in the living room for tea.'

Subcommander Sorgue had promised a seamless transition to democracy, and it was so. Of the twenty-odd citizens who had decided to run for president, only Doualé Bocandé enjoyed unimpeachable street cred. Everyone in the entire country owned at least one cassette, dating back to the time of General Mansaré, of the famous griot defying the powers that be with 'Coupez Coupez,' a seditious anthem that was copied and recopied to make more copies that were then copied and recopied again. The haunting power of her voice withstood this generational decay and defied the usual lifespan of magnetic tape. The accompaniment on the balafon and mbëng-mbëng, however catchy, could in such a context never hope to play more than a supporting role.

And so it went, for the first year of Doualé Bocandé's presidency. The Grande Dame announced a massive irrigation project for both sides of the great river, nationalized the diamond mines, opened schools, instituted a minimum wage, criminalized domestic violence, resuscitated the peanut industry, founded a tribunal on religious matters, and much more besides. Building the new international airport, and the highway to service it, won her the support of the opposition, a loose coalition of merchants and lawyers more than happy to do business with this formidable socialist. Even the right-wing newspapers came around. As for the support of the people, it was universal (within the margin of error of polling methods, particularly in rural areas).

Simone saw it all take shape up close. She'd arrived in Port Merveille by sea, emergency visa in hand, just a few months before the election. A civil servant had been waiting to drive her to the Presidential Palace. There Simone dropped an innocuous cloth bag onto Subcommander Sorgue's desk.

A nod of the military man's large, weary head silently confirmed the presence of the Supreme Orchestra within. He closed the bag and passed it to a subordinate.

'Madame,' he stated in a grave voice, 'we know what a heavy price you paid to bring us this treasure. Our nation is forever deeply in your debt.'

Once in her hotel room, Simone spread out her meagre possessions. In her haste, she had brought along three copies of *Ballerina Porteña*, which she'd received just before leaving. But the square book with her name on the cover now seemed like an ancient artifact of a life that was no longer hers. Exhausted, she slept.

In the days that followed, Simone ventured out into the city and took dazed, disoriented walks, as if thrust outside the world. A deafening sun leaned down over these leisurely walks. The noisy streets of the metropolis were illegible; their teeming action made her dizzy; she didn't understand a word spoken by the merchants; the olfactory palette of fish and gasoline did nothing to alleviate her vertigo. She ended up taking her custom to the Café des Aristos, near the old fire station, where she discovered the art of tea. She visited the Musée national des arts, a modern and impressively large building she was disappointed to find decrepit and emptied out by years under the rule of a backward dictatorship. One afternoon she bought two pagnes, one yellow and green, the other pink, grey, and blue, but back in her room she did little more than stare at them, as she had no idea how to tie them as the locals did. Finally, overtaken by acute homesickness, she collapsed onto the too-soft bed.

The next morning, visitors were waiting for Simone in the hotel lobby. Mariama Coly, a civil servant who had been named Head of Public Works for the new republic, was there at Subcommander Sorgue's behest. The two women climbed into a black four-by-four and left the city, via a rough road over bush that passed through several villages. A gris-gris hung from the rear-view mirror. Mariama

Coly wore black glasses and steered with a ring-studded hand, flashing a huge smile at anything that crossed her path. 'You'll see,' she said from time to time, almost enviously, 'what it means to get the royal treatment.'

The colonial house with yellow walls and blue shutters had been unoccupied since the departure of its owner, a wealthy foreigner who was compromised at the highest level and decamped at the first confirmation of General Mansaré's overthrow. The state, Mariam Coly explained, had seized a large number of residences abandoned by mysteriously indisposed sympathizers of the previous regime.

'My dear friend of democracy,' stated the public servant, 'I hope you will accept this gift from our young republic.'

The house was a pretty one, it's true, and would be even more so with a little work. Simone hadn't expected such generosity from her hosts. True, she'd delivered the diamond. It was the least she could do. And then she'd felt the need to lie low a while. Port Merveille had seemed as good a place as any. Simone opened the shutters of the window that gave onto the backyard, whose tree branches housed a flock of quelea. A few hundred metres away, the great river flowed by, dotted with pirogues and small fishing boats. Clusters of women and children were hard at work along the banks. Simone turned and stuttered out her heartfelt thanks.

'Subcommander Sorgue would like to know,' continued Mariama Coly of the inexhaustible courtesy, 'if you would also do us the honour of accepting a position in one of our ministries.'

'Well,' answered Simone, 'I don't know.'

'What do you know how to do?'

'I'm an artist,' Simone confessed.

'No one's perfect!' quipped Mariama Coly, with a guffaw.

The election of Doualé Bocandé had unleashed nationwide jubilation. On that historic night, Simone, who was still acclimatizing, had gone to a village café where the television was relaying the election results at full blast. A cacophony of incredulous, joyful shouts rose up at the announcement of the first-round victory. The winner's speech brought warm tears to Simone's eyes. Never before had a political event moved her thus.

A few days later, the president announced the makeup of her cabinet: mostly members of the social-democratic coalition, with a handful of moderate Muslims. Non-elected citizens would get key portfolios: Subcommander Sorgue stayed at the helm of the Armed Forces; a doctor was grafted onto the Ministry of Health; a rehabilitated henchmen of General Mansaré got Transport as a consolation prize.

Simone, with her newspaper open in front of her, went through this list of unknown names, illustrated with dignified portraits. After working her way down to the Minister of Culture, Simone was stunned. No way! It couldn't be. She rubbed her eyes, put her reading glasses back on, took another look, reread the name of the freshly appointed minister, who the newspaper did not fail to mention with a scarcely repressed amazement was the granddaughter of General Mansaré, recently returned to her homeland after years of exile and study far from the influence of her reviled patriarch. The young woman was a partisan of the honourable team, and promised now to give everyone cause to forget forever the dark years in which culture was held in neglect by the cretinous former administration.

There could be no doubt: Simone would have recognized that face in a crowd of thousands. It was Faya.

Simone had no difficulty learning to ride the scooter she climbed onto every morning to go to town. In the end she'd accepted one of the government positions offered her: interim head of the Musée national des arts. She soon discovered that her pay was far from handsome. But it was a little pocket money, and a break from the routine.

Her predecessor had bequeathed her an office gone to seed and account books not updated in a decade. The state of the collections wasn't much better: ancient pieces lived out their dotage tossed in with tondos and statues and colonial photographs. The conservation team was two young interns who'd escaped the University of Port Merveille, allegedly supervised by one Sow, whose existence Simone had so far been unable to confirm. The two interns were put to work establishing some order in the storage rooms, ensuring every piece was recorded in the museum register, and setting aside items that needed to be restored. By cross-checking storage rooms against registers, Simone discovered that many pieces had gone missing, and not minor ones either: the previous director had taken advantage of the generalized corruption under General Mansaré's administration to fatten his wallet, with the help of customs officers not above dipping their feet into the swamp.

Less than a month after taking office, Simone submitted to the ministry a lengthy list of her needs: people would have to be hired, a budget allocated, ties forged with foreign museums, retrospectives of local artists held. The building itself needed renovations. A few weeks later she got word that the Minister of Culture wished to see her.

Simone arrived a little late: it was easy to get lost in Port Merveille's unlabelled streets. With her helmet under one arm and a copy of her report under the other, she entered a former trading post in the port district, now home to a few minor ministries, including Culture. The hallways were almost devoid of people. Simone found the office on her own. She went in a door on the top floor, where she was kept waiting by a secretary until Madame the Minister was available; and available she was, a few short minutes later.

It's always awkward being reunited with someone you once shared bedsheets with. But Faya was a public figure now. No sooner had Simone entered than Faya opened her arms in a presidential welcome and placed consecrating hands on Simone's shoulders. She wore a long, elegant green-and-ochre pagne, and a scarf of the same pattern covered her hair. In Port Merveille, her skin was considered pale and her accent was de-Westernizing rapidly. Faya invited Simone to sit, and did the same on the other side of the desk. 'So I hear you're interim director of our museum,' said the minister. Simone shrugged her shoulders as we all do to evoke the unpredictability of fate.

'I've read through your report,' said Faya, flipping through the document in question. 'Nice work. It'll be useful when the time comes to make decisions. But let me make one thing clear upfront: you'll have to find other funding sources. Everyone has their hands in the government's pockets – everyone! I just came from a meeting with our National Film Board. They'd happily swallow up our entire budget on their own! Luckily, our president is a champion of culture. So not everything is lost. And of course, as our beloved director, you must realize there is foreign aid available to a country like ours. Our cultural heritage has been pillaged shamelessly these last years, and today graces museums all over the world. It's time to pull some strings, begin applying to international organizations. I'll provide names and addresses. As for the renovations,' she added, turning the pages as if to remind herself, 'the project is of interest to my colleague in Public Works. He mentioned foreign investors.'

'And my conservators?' asked Simone, understanding that her pecuniary demands were unlikely to be met.

'Listen, Madame Director, we can't print money on demand. But you are lucky: Minister Sorgue likes you, and by extension so does the president. Your conservators will have a salary. A civil servant's salary,' she said apologetically.

'They'll appreciate that, I'm sure,' said Simone, who could well imagine its paltriness.

Faya then put on a serious look.

'Madame Director,' she began, choosing her words with care. 'You aren't from around here. But you'll have to come to terms, and soon, with the priorities of our president. Our people have been held down; the time has now come to lift them up, rekindle their pride. As we speak, we are looking into several monumental projects that will instill a sense of national pride. Your museum must be part of this current. We are laying the groundwork for a great reckoning. We have to keep our eyes on the big picture. Do a lot with a little: that's been our people's talent since time immemorial. Because foreign capital never does more than pass through. It never stays long, my dear Simone. At best, we get a few crumbs. We're tired of gathering crumbs. It's time to bake our own bread.'

An astonished Simone let herself be swept along by her old friend's nationalist fervour. This *great reckoning* must have been in her since she was old enough to understand how the world worked. Faya's formidable selfishness didn't preclude a keen feeling for injustice against others, which she denounced as the strong preying on the weak and the violence inherent in all forms of submission; in fact, that narcissistic obstinacy was now feeding this flowery grandiloquence so befitting of a Minister of Culture. Simone would have to do a lot with a little. In this country, she had no choice. But then, she had always been well-versed in the art of constructing worlds on scraps of paper.

Pierre-Luc came bearing news from the old country. Christiane Chorbat was single again; Isabeau de Milicieux was opening a second vintage-clothing shop; Poupée Sincère's old singer had rejoined the group, definitively finished with her studies in agronomy. His new job with Alban Wouters – who by the way sent Simone his regards – had immersed Pierre-Luc in the tiny contemporary art world, a subject of interest to the interim director of the Musée national des arts. Pierre-Luc rattled off a few artists' names, which Simone noted down for future reference.

'Esma Lorca,' Pierre-Luc ventured. 'A friend of yours, no?'

'Esma Lorca,' Simone confirmed, at the mention of the tattoo artist's name. 'Whatever is she up to?'

'She's organizing performances. Kind of like fashion shows. Men only, tattooed by her exclusively. It's blowing up. Alban's turning people away at the door.'

'So they walk the catwalk ... naked?'

'How else?' asked Pierre-Luc.

Simone looked at her old friend with curiosity. There was something different about him, something fundamentally changed. He radiated confidence when he spoke, and she'd never seen him so relaxed. Sarah-Jeanne Loubier was also possessed of a newfound assurance; expressing herself without a trace of deference, she was now fully at home in the role of the artist, unburdened of false modesty. Their age difference barely showed now. It was as if they'd met halfway.

'You're forgetting Alban's message,' Sarah-Jeanne reminded Pierre-Luc without lifting her eyes from the sketch she was working on as they caught up.

'You're right,' said Pierre-Luc. 'Alban wants to know if you have new work for him.'

Simone sighed and shrugged her shoulders.

'I don't really draw anymore.'

On that note, Sarah-Jeanne Loubier put down her sketchbook, revealing a lovely if unfinished portrait of Simone.

'If that's true, it's a shame,' said Sarah-Jeanne Loubier.

'It will come back to you. No doubt,' said Pierre-Luc, with an encouraging smile.

'I guess so,' Simone lied. 'Hey, how about going out to eat in town? I know a place with great caldou.'

She called a seven-seater. At eight o'clock, they pulled into Port Merveille in all its splendour, as the sun went down over the docks. Everyone loved the fish stew, even Pierre-Luc who didn't always get along with seafood. The heat was dropping lazily. They slipped between the stalls of the market that stayed open round the clock. At one of them Simone ordered cold drinks, which they enjoyed on an ad hoc outdoor terrace at the corner of the square. Sarah-Jeanne had put down her sketchbook for the moment. A woman passed by, in a yellow batik pagne depicting President Bocandé encircled in palm fronds. A radio station played in the background. They laughed over little nothings.

'And what about those bags we picked up at the left-luggage office?' Sarah-Jeanne Loubier asked suddenly. 'Did they make it into the right hands?'

'The embassy took care of it,' Simone confirmed. 'That was nice of you to do me that favour. And let me pass on the effusive thanks of the Minister of Finance.'

'That's what you could call having your cake and eating it too,' Pierre-Luc said philosophically, having realized exactly what had happened.

'Still, it's too bad about Charles ...' said Sarah-Jeanne, on a more sombre note.

Simone shrugged her shoulders. Everything had happened so fast, that day at the station. She'd been hauled in by the police, conditionally released not long after. Then came three interminable days of waiting, until the two men in putty-coloured raincoats appeared and informed her somewhat coldly that Charles Rose was now, in the official government records, deceased. No funeral, no burial, no publicity around the body. One simple stipulation: you must accept what we are telling you. Dead? Impossible. How could one be dead?

And then Charles Rose's mission was completed. He may not have delivered the diamond to its final destination, but Simone knew where it was: concealed in one of the cylinders of the lighting fixture in the apartment of her deceased fourth husband. And since she also had the key ...

'The shortest of my marriages,' she said in summary, concealing for better or for worse her grief. 'But let's not put a damper on our night. Are you guys up for more? How about a little dancing?'

It wouldn't do to visit Port Merveille without going dancing at least once in the Briqueterie district, where waves of jubilant merrymakers wash up nightly, drawn by the deafening rhythms of refrains ringing out from hangars whose whitewashed walls are painted with unforgettable signs. Inside, revellers are greeted by scarf-wrapped speakers pounding out sounds from all over the spectrum and an embarrassment of neon lighting around which small swarms of flies buzz, and a wet heat wins the battle against hapless pedestal fans. Here, in the midst of young men dressed in polos and white pants and shod in borrowed brogues, and young ladies whose thin dresses billow up above stiletto heels, and hype men rocking panamas and trilbies, dress shirts, and patterned bell-bottoms, and girls with nappy hair whose pagnes twirl triumphantly around their flesh, you join an intrepid throng of dancers whose feet tread the tile with an unstudied grace born of the coming of night after a long day of labour, a crowd periodically galvanized afresh by the cries of the DJs, the raucous night kept impenitently aloft until the first rosy fingers of dawn appear.

Sarah-Jeanne threw herself onto the dance floor without hesitation; Pierre-Luc cut loose with total abandon; Simone kicked back on one of the rare chairs, taking occasional sips of her beer.

Earlier that morning she had watched her friends napping, almost naked, in the large bed in the backroom, hands interlaced. Simone's eye came to rest on the scene for a mere fraction of a second, and she fell into a reverie of their intimate commerce. There was something in it that partook of the sweetness of forbidden fruit, and it inspired a joyful jealousy in her. Butterflies tickled her stomach. She followed their example and retreated to her bed. But sleep did not come. To think that she had known Pierre-Luc only in his almost caricatured clumsiness, and Sarah-Jeanne Loubier in the prison of her shyness ... Love, she thought, transforms us, or some of us at least. And it was stronger than she. Now it was this pair, in their togetherness, that she desired.

As was often the case, Alice Mansaré still had on her lab coat when she left the Institute of Neurology, affiliated with the University of Neudorf, and found her car in the public parking lot across the street. It was fall, but the sun was shining and her heart was light. The idea of returning home pleased her. She left the old city, took a tunnel, and merged onto the Périphérique.

Since her divorce from Doctor Fliess a few years back, she'd resumed the habits of her earlier, single self: staying late at the lab, eating out, coming home just to sleep, at least when she wasn't invited to some distant conference. One doesn't become the leading specialist in concurrent forms of aytpical trigeminal neuralgia without periodically sacrificing oneself for such missions, which sometimes left, it must be said, a little time for sightseeing. This new lifestyle had been exacerbated by the departure of Eugénie, her only daughter, who was, after all, old enough to leave the nest and had at any rate never done anything other than exactly what she felt like, ever since she was a little girl.

Then there had been, a few weeks earlier at a café by the city walls, that secret rendezvous with a gentleman whose features were strained by worry and who claimed to be in the employ of a foreign agency which, under the circumstances, he wasn't eager to name. The worried gentleman was retiring in a few days, which would be none too soon, and before he did he wished to inform Alice Mansaré of certain affairs likely to interest her. Did she know, for example, that her only daughter, who was no longer going by the name Eugénie, had been living in Bruant, where she'd gotten into a few scrapes that had all been resolved in the end? It was nothing to worry about. 'I wasn't worried in the least,' Alice Mansaré informed the worried gentlemen, whose index and right thumb rubbed a preoccupied temple, and who proceeded to mumble a few thoughts on the reckless shenanigans of certain of his subordinates and the reliability of the Service's cybernetics squad more generally, then alluded to an enemy agent whose electronic brain had had to be infiltrated, as well as certain pop songs that had, upon further analysis, proven in fact to be coded messages addressed to the enemy – such are the times, no? Alice Mansaré, eager to understand the finer points, tried to relate them to the vicissitudes of her own field. 'Have you been following the news in Port Merveille these last few weeks?' the man added. 'Your daughter has a surprise in store for you.' 'I know,' Alice Mansaré answered.

Here the worried gentleman, who had finally been served a glass of water with which to swallow his two extra-strength antacid tablets, had a small favour to ask of Alice Mansaré. It concerned, he explained, a person she knew intimately, who had been a touch too much in the spotlight recently, and would she agree to take this person in for a few days, away from the prying eyes, if she took his meaning. Alice Mansaré did. 'This whole story must seem frightfully confusing,' apologized the worried man before taking his leave. 'Not at all,' answered Alice Mansaré, 'it's crystal clear.'

It was a phrase she could not apply to the Périphérique, where heavy traffic had slowed to a crawl.

As she came through the door that evening, Alice Mansaré recognized the aroma of peanut nététou floating through the empty kitchen. In the pot there simmered a stew whose incomparable bouquet summoned forth Alice's childhood memories from before the separation … before the exile. It was a dish Maguette had made her young charges all the time.

'Mafé chicken,' she said approvingly, lifting up the lid.

A paradise lost may be lost forever, she thought (we think, we all think – such is our lot), and nothing ever remains of our deepest secrets once we abandon them, under duress or of our own volition. Nothing less than a spell is required to bring them back.

Yet this lost homeland, this joyous time past, was also a time out of law, a province of an ungoverned country.

Alice Mansaré locked the double door and drew the curtains of every main-floor window. She let down her hair, set her glasses on the night table, got undressed, put on a robe. She walked, barefoot, to the bathroom, knocked three times, and gently opened the door. A warm puff of steam wafted through the opening, along with the scent of olive-oil soap. In the clawfoot tub, her brother was lounging. Yes, she noticed, the spell still held.

At the sight of his big sister, Fabrice Mansaré was intoxicated. He unfolded his legs. 'Coming in?' he asked. She let her robe drop on the tiled floor and joined him in the almost boiling water. They exchanged a fraught look, as if emerging simultaneously from a long reverie. Her skin had copper highlights, there were green flashes in her eyes. His appearance was a titch less appealing, with the scars that striped his side, but the contusions were getting less serious every day. They held hands underwater, stomachs aflutter. 'All right, little brother, I've taken the rest of the week off.' He nodded in agreement. And then they stopped speaking altogether.

About the Translator

Pablo Strauss grew up in British Columbia and now makes his home in Quebec City. He has translated several works of fiction from Quebec, including Maxime Raymond Bock's *Baloney* (Coach House Books, 2016).

The translator thanks the author for his assistance, editor Alana Wilcox, and Mary Thaler for her invaluable first edit of this translation.

About the Author

David Turgeon is the author of four novels, *Simone au travail* (translated as *The Supreme Orchestra*), *Le continent de plastique* (finalist, Prix littéraire des collégiens), *La revanche de l'écrivaine fantôme*, and *Les bases secrètes*. He has also published several graphic novels, a collection of essays on comics, and, most recently, *À propos du style de Genette*, a non-fiction meditation on the French theorist's literary style (Le Quartanier, 2018). David Turgeon is a founding member of *Tristesse* magazine. He lives in Montreal.

Typeset in Albertina.

Printed at the Coach House on bpNichol Lane in Toronto, Ontario,
on Zephyr Antique Laid paper, which was manufactured, acid-free,
in Saint-Jérôme, Quebec, from second-growth forests. This book
was printed with vegetable-based ink on a 1973 Heidelberg KORD
offset litho press. Its pages were folded on a Baumfolder, gathered
by hand, bound on a Sulby Auto-Minabinda, and trimmed on a Polar
single-knife cutter.

Translated by Pablo Strauss
Edited and designed by Alana Wilcox
Cover by Ingrid Paulson

Coach House Books
80 bpNichol Lane
Toronto ON M5S 3J4
Canada

416 979 2217
800 367 6360

mail@chbooks.com
www.chbooks.com